DAMIEN—OMEN II

The prophecy from the darkest vision of evil
is now coming true!

Also available:

Joseph Howard

Damien—Omen II

from the screenplay by
Stanley Mann and Michael Hodges

Futura Publications Limited
A Futura Book

A Futura Book

First published in Great Britain by
Futura Publications Limited in 1978
Reprinted 1978

NOTE
In the original novel, *The Omen*, the first name of Ambassador
Thorn was given as 'Jeremy'. In the film, his name was
changed to 'Robert'. As the film *Damien – Omen II* retains
'Robert', this book does the same.

ISBN 0 7088 1358 5

Printed in Great Britain by
Hazell Watson & Viney Ltd
Aylesbury, Bucks

Futura Publications Limited,
110 Warner Road,
Camberwell, London SE5

PROLOGUE:

SEVEN YEARS AGO

Carl Bugenhagen, the archaeologist, was worried.

Not because he was deep down under the ground, burrowing around like a mole in a hole. Bugenhagen liked it down there. It was cool, and dark, and it smelled pleasantly of the past, and it was quiet. Except for now.

Bugenhagen had begun to hear sounds.

Bugenhagen was not easily frightened. He was a powerful man in his late fifties, with the huge neck and shoulders of a classic Greek wrestler. His white hair and beard and his wild eyes gave him the look of an Old Testament prophet, which was appropriate since, at this very moment, Bugenhagen was exploring an excavation, under the surface of Israel. He was there not only because he was one of the world's foremost archaeologists, but also because he was trying to prove the existence of the Devil.

The sounds alarmed Bugenhagen, and he had good reason to be afraid. He suspected he was the next in a series of people the Devil had been forced to kill because they threatened to expose the truth. Moreover, the Devil had excellent reason to kill Bugenhagen, for Bugenhagen, in his pride and in his piety, had attempted to kill *Him*.

Bugenhagen was not trying to find evidence to prove the existence of the Devil to himself; he had all the proof he needed – in fact, all he could bear. Everything he had suspected for so long had turned out to be absolutely true. Terrifyingly so. No – he needed the proof for his associate, Michael Morgon, so that the truth could live on. Bugenhagen know only too well that one who had tried to kill the Anti-Christ – and failed – could not hope to escape punishment.

Bugenhagen had first broached the subject with Morgan the day before, as they sat drinking sweet liqueurs in a charming seaside café and watching the late afternoon shadows stretch out along the cooling tile floor beneath their feet . . .

At first Morgan didn't believe him. Bugenhagen could understand why. It did take some adjustment. As he sat in that Middle Eastern world of bright colors, the setting sun shooting deep oranges and reds over the dark blue Mediterranean, and the softening light reflecting off the white stone walls of the old Israeli city of Acre, even Bugenhagen considered for the first time the possibility that he might be stark, raving mad.

But then something inside him, some voice that didn't seem to be any voice he recognized, assured him that not only was he sane, he was *blessed* with a knowledge that was his enormous responsibility to impart.

It bothered Bugenhagen that while Morgan remained understandably skeptical, Morgan's attractive girl friend had no trouble believing him. That she was even with them had bothered Bugenhagen to begin with, but Morgan was an incorrigible romantic and rarely without a woman, no matter what the occasion. So even though Bugenhagen had expressly insisted upon a private meeting, he was not at all surprised to find a woman with Morgan – just annoyed.

Her name was Joan Hart, and she was very striking, with auburn hair and flashing eyes. Bugenhagen didn't know what to make of women like her. When he was younger, young enough to have been swayed by her looks, though certainly not by the way she talked, women like Joan Hart didn't even exist.

She was a free-lance photo-journalist, a fact she not only announced at every opportunity, underscoring it by a firm handshake and a professional smile, but which she further accented by the manner in which she dressed. Her outfit, which had obviously been custom-made by a London tailor, at a no doubt exorbitant price, was apparently designed to recall Ernest Hemingway on safari. She wore absurdly oversized jewelry and was never without several Nikons slung around her neck. She smoked and talked incessantly.

But for all her paraphernalia, Joan Hart was not in Acre entirely because of an assignment. She was there because of Michael Morgan, who was, at the moment, the most important man in her life, though it was true that her work claimed all of the interest and attention that Michael Morgan did not.

Joan Hart, who had just arrived by plane from her home base in London, had already seen the newspaper headline that Bugenhagen was now showing Morgan:

U.S. AMBASSADOR AND WIFE BURIED.

Morgan had already seen it too, although he hadn't been very interested in it at the time, nor for that matter was he interested in it now.

'Yes,' he said in that detached manner that only upper-class Englishmen can muster when they are trying to be polite, 'very curious.'

Bugenhagen, undaunted, showed him the other newspaper, the American one, with the headline:

PRESIDENT AND WIFE COMFORT AMBASSADOR'S BEREAVED SON.

Bugenhagen pointed with his stubby finger at the photograph of a six-year-old boy with a black armband on his sleeve, a boy with a face as beautiful and radiant as the faces of the cherubim the Renaissance painters used to put in the corners of their church ceilings, up high where no one could see.

'Don't you recognize him?' asked Bugenhagen.

7

Morgan looked at the picture again, studying it more closely this time. 'No,' he said finally.

The frustration of being the only one left who knew, the only one left who understood, was starting to take its toll on Bugenhagen. He spoke more sharply than he intended. 'Haven't you seen Yigael's Wall yet?' he asked.

'They only uncovered it last week, Carl,' Morgan started to say, but Bugenhagen interrupted. The need to explain it once and for all, no matter how wild and illogical it sounded, was all that Bugenhagen could think of. *There was so little time.* He stabbed at the photograph again, and said very slowly and very distinctly: 'The face of Yigael's Satan is the same! There is no doubt! This boy, this "Damien Thorn," is the *Anti-Christ*!'

Morgan raised an eyebrow in bemused protest. 'Carl –' he began, but Bugenhagen interrupted him again.

'You must believe me!'

Morgan stopped smiling. The intensity in Bugenhagen's face suddenly frightened him. This was no doddering old fool; this was his mentor, the man who had taught him everything he knew. 'Carl,' he began again, more softly this time, not quite knowing what he was going to say next. 'I'm an archaeologist, not a religious fanatic.'

Bugenhagen persisted. 'Whereof ye have *heard* that he should come . . .' But then he couldn't remember the rest. He was so tired. He hadn't slept in days. He'd been afraid to. And now his memory was starting to fail him.

Morgan glanced at Joan, but saw instantly that he would get no help from her. She was absolutely mesmerized by Bugenhagen's performance. He shook his head and turned back to Bugenhagen. 'What are the *facts*, Carl?'

Bugenhagen lifted his head. 'A week ago,' he said, 'his father tried to kill him. On the altar of All Saints Church in London. He tried to drive some daggers through the boy's heart.'

Joan shuddered with morbid excitement. Morgan reached for his drink as he glanced through the newspaper clippings again. 'There's one minor detail these papers seem to have omitted,' he said.

Bugenhagen took a deep breath, then said, 'I gave him the daggers myself. My friend Father James was there at All Saints and witnessed the whole thing. He made a special call to tell me what happened. He recognized the ancient daggers and persuaded the American Embassy to retrieve them from the police for return to me.'

In the long silence that followed, Morgan just stared at him, his drink forgotten halfway to his mouth. Joan's gaze was riveted on him. Bugenhagen knew he had their attention now, and he went on, speaking forcefully and rapidly, trying to get it all in while the shock of his statement still had them trapped.

'The Ambassador's name was Robert Thorn,' he said. 'When his wife lost a baby in a hospital in Rome, he took a newborn child at the urging of a man who was posing as a priest, but who was, in fact, an Apostle of the Beast. Thorn gave the child to his wife before she knew her own had died, leading her to believe it *was* her own. They loved the child and brought it up in London – not knowing it was born of a jackal!' Bugenhagen paused to swallow before going on. 'Soon it began to destroy all those who awakened to its true nature, and Thorn came to me for help. I listened to his story and knew instantly that he spoke the truth, for I had long been receiving signs that I would one day be the one who would have to act. I gave Thorn the seven ancient daggers that are the necessary weapons to drive through the Devil's heart. By then, Thorn's wife was dead, as were two other poor souls who had learned the truth.' Bugenhagen bowed his head. 'Before Thorn could pierce the foul heart of his Devil-son, the police killed him, thinking he was mad from grief following the death of his wife!' Bugenhagen then paused to point to the photograph again. This was the one thing he wanted Morgan to comprehend and to act upon: '*The child still lives*!'

After a very long time, Morgan asked, 'Where is he now?'

'In America,' answered Bugenhagen, 'living with his uncle, his father's brother. Where, as it is written, "His power shall be mighty; and he shall destroy wonderfully, and shall prosper, and practice, and destroy the mighty and the holy." '

Joan Hart, ever the journalist, was beside herself. 'Oh, Michael,' she said, 'let's go to America!'

'Shut up!' Michael told her. This was no mere newspaper scoop. If anything that Bugenhagen had just said was true, this was nothing to take lightly.

Bugenhagen reached down at his feet and picked up a wonderfully intricate old leather pouch fitted out with several pockets and many straps and buckles. It clanked as he placed it on the table.

'You must take this to the boy's new parents,' he said. 'Inside are the daggers, as well as a letter explaining everything.'

Morgan thought about what Bugenhagen wanted him to do. It was one thing to hear the story from someone who was convinced of the facts and to be moved by the power of his delivery; it was quite another thing to spread the story yourself.

'I'm sorry, Carl,' he said, shaking his head. 'You can't expect me to just . . .'

'They have to be warned!' Bugenhagen cried. The people at the next table turned their heads in irritation. Bugenhagen lowered his voice to a hoarse whisper. 'I'm too old, too ill,' he said. 'I can't go myself. And since I'm the only person who knows the truth, I must . . .' Bugenhagen evidently found the thought so frightening that he was unable to say it aloud.

'Must what?' Morgan prompted him.

Bugenhagen stared into his drink. '. . . Stay where I'll be safe,' he said.

Morgan shook his head sadly. 'My dear friend,' he sighed. Bugenhagen knew what Morgan was going to say even before he said it. He recognized the condescending tone in his voice. 'I have a reputation,' Morgan went on, but Bugenhagen overrode him vehemently: 'That's why it *has* to be you! They'll listen to you!'

Morgan was becoming unnerved. There was something unsettling about Bugenhagen's fervor, but what he was asking Morgan to do was simply impossible. 'C'mon, Carl,' he said, 'they'd have me committed.'

Bugenhagen stood up. With the light from the setting sun behind him outlining his prophet's beard, he looked fierce, mad, and holy. 'Come to Yigael's Wall,' he said. It was a command, unlike any command Morgan had ever heard before. There was no resisting it.

'Now?' he asked quietly, already knowing what the answer would be.

'Now,' said Bugenhagen, and he turned and walked outside to his jeep.

Joan felt excluded. 'May I come too?' she asked, putting on her most winning smile.

Morgan shook his head. 'Why don't you wait for me back at the hotel? This won't take long.' He leaned forward and gave her a long, lingering kiss. Then he got up to leave.

'All right,' she said with an exaggerated sigh of impatience. 'But I'm telling you now – I won't wait forever.'

He laughed and blew her another kiss, then disappeared around the corner.

And that was the last time Joan Hart ever saw Michael Morgan, although it took her a long time to accept it, and an even longer time to understand why.

The ancient walled castle of Belvoir stood at the head

of the Cebulan Valley, not far from the city of Acre. It had been there since the twelfth century, when the Crusaders, whose name derived from the cross of Christ, came down from Europe to wrest the Holy Land from the Moslems. They built the castle in His name. And it was in the ruins of the castle that Bugenhagen found the proof he needed — that an Anti-Christ was living among us. *Now.*

Long-haired sheep were grazing among the decaying walls and arches when the distant rumble of a jeep caused them to raise their heads and twitch their ears in the direction of the disturbing sound. Dawn was breaking; the sun rose livid red above the valley, sending long multi-colored shadows streaking across the landscape. When the jeep suddenly emerged over the top of the nearest hill, and began to barrel down in their direction, the sheep stumbled and scattered, their bells clanging discordantly, as if summoning supplicants to a travesty of prayer.

The jeep pulled up close to the ruined castle wall, and Bugenhagen and Morgan got out. It was cold in the early morning air, but only Morgan seemed to notice or to care. Bugenhagen was intent on digging up an extra miner's helmet out of the pile of equipment in the back of the jeep. Where they were going, *both* of them would need helmets. It was too dark to rely on the light of only one lamp, and too dangerous to attempt without some protection for the head.

What both men failed to notice was a large black raven, which perched on the highest part of the wall and watched them with blank, malevolent eyes.

Bugenhagen and Morgan walked across the vast, dark banquet hall of the castle, past the six fifty-foot pillars that ran the length of the chamber. Sleeping bats hung from the eaves. The old man clutched the leather pouch to his chest, as though he were fearful to be separated from it. Both men switched on their headlamps and began the descent down the time-worn steps into the subterranean recesses of the archaeological dig.

Others had been there not long before. Boards had been laid where the most recent excavations had been dug, to facilitate crossing the mud and the ditches. Modern equipment and ancient discoveries lined the walls, lying incongruously side by side, both covered by the same impersonal plastic.

And then Morgan saw something that nearly made him jump out of his skin – a carving at once so obscene and so seductively beautiful that it made him gasp. It was a statue of a woman sitting upon a scarlet Beast. The Beast had seven hideous heads and ten awful horns and was covered with words carved in languages no one had spoken for thousands of years.

Morgan may have been a skeptic, but he was not a fool. He knew exactly what he was looking at. 'The Whore of Babylon,' he said aloud. The terrible name echoed off the walls.

He looked up only to see Bugenhagen disappear through an opening in the wall. Bugenhagen hadn't heard him. Morgan shuddered involuntarily and went after him. He had no intention of being stranded alone in the dark with the dreadful statue of the Whore of Babylon. He followed Bugenhagen into the next chamber.

And there it was. Yigael's Wall. Bugenhagen's headlamp flashed over the work of an artist who had been driven to madness – and genius – when confronted night after night by the terrible and ever-changing face of Satan.

In the largest picture, Satan was in his awesome maturity, having already been cast down into Chaos. He was shown clinging to the side of a precipice, his muscular arms and legs straining from the terrible effort, his enormous batlike wings spread wide to protect him. His face was chipped away and not clearly defined.

There was a second portrait, full-face with forked-tongued serpents writhing out of the scalp instead of hair. This face, too, seemed oddly undefined and vague.

But there was yet another portrait, a smaller one – Satan as a child. In this picture, the face was as clear as could be. It was a face as beautiful as that of a Renaissance cherub. It was also the face of the boy in the newspaper photograph. It was the face of Damien Thorn.

'This will convince you,' Bugenhagen said, but Morgan was already convinced.

As he moved toward the wall, fascinated, pulled by the power of the portrait, a sound like the crack of a bullwhip suddenly shot down the tunnel, followed by a deep and terrifying rumble. Morgan stumbled back toward Bugenhagen. The two men stood absolutely still and waited. An eternity of seconds ticked by.

And then the tunnel roof in front of them suddenly gave way and began crashing down in an avalanche of stone and dirt. The dust rose in thick, swirling clouds, and Morgan started to choke. Bugenhagen remained calm. When Morgan's racking coughing had subsided, he turned to Bugenhagen and asked, 'Is there another way out?'

Bugenhagen shook his head, and it was then that Bugenhagen began to feel terror. He understood why this was happening, and in the same instant he knew there was nothing they could do about it.

There was another earsplitting crack, and another rumble, and the roof behind them caved in. The space in the tunnel was now no more than five feet wide. It had become their tomb.

In the deathly silence that followed, Morgan looked at Bugenhagen in horror. The old man's eyes were already closed in resignation. He was preparing to die.

And then there came a new sound: quiet, sinister, as persistent as doom. At first, Morgan didn't recognize it, but then he saw a steady stream of sand trickling down from one tiny hole in the ceiling. And then there were two holes. Then four. Then twelve. Soon it was raining sand. The sand sifted into their eyes and their mouths; it piled up over the tops of their boots.

Morgan finally realized that he was about to die. He looked down; and there at his feet lay the Whore of Babylon. The falling sand had already begun to cover the statue. Although he knew it was pointless, Morgan began to claw wildly at the rubble. His knuckles and fingertips started to bleed, and he began to cry.

'The Anti-Christ is with us!' shouted Bugenhagen, through the rasping of the pouring sand. 'Give yourself to God!'

Outside, as if in blasphemous answer, the walls and the pillars of the castle lurched and began to crumble. Down below, the rumbling was amplified into a terrifying roar. Morgan began to moan as he continued to claw away at the wall of stone that stood between him and his only chance for survival. But the sand was already up to his waist, and rising fast.

Bugenhagen's eyes were still closed. He was praying: ' ". . . and he had power to give life unto the image of the Beast; that the image of the Beast should both speak and cause that as many as would *not* worship the image of the Beast should be killed." ' Bugenhagen paused, then added, 'Bless us, Christ Jesus, and forgive us . . .'

The sand was at the level of their chins now. Morgan was whimpering like a frightened animal. Bugenhagen kept praying:

' ". . . the forces of evil may seem to overwhelm us and be triumphant, but *goodness will prevail*. For it is written in the Book of Revelation: '. . . and then shall that wicked one be revealed, whom the Lord shall consume with the spirit of His mouth, and shall destroy with the brightness of His coming . . .' " '

The sand rose over their mouths, and over their noses, and over their eyes, and when it moved up over their foreheads, their headlamps were extinguished in a single terrible moment, leaving the black void, the absence of everything, that is death.

A final, thunderous lurch sent the rest of the ruined castle down to the ground in a roaring cascade of flying rubble and stone.

Two things remained. The wall by the mad painter Yigael – the single solid piece of evidence left – had somehow miraculously survived intact. And lying next to it, in the rubble far below the surface of the earth, was Bugenhagen's leather pouch. It was as if some *other* force, equally as powerful as that depicted on the wall, were at work, leaving evidence of its presence.

On the surface of the earth, out of the mushrooming cloud of dust and debris, the raven soared mightily, like a blackened phoenix rising from the ashes. It circled the ruins below with a hideous, triumphant shriek, then flew off into the rising sun, and disappeared into the early morning mist.

CHAPTER ONE

The boy's face glowed brightly in the light of the crackling flames. It was a handsome face, though overly serious for someone not quite thirteen. The eyes were intent and brooding now, as they stared through the closing dusk at the bonfire's flames. He was trying to remember. A primitive ache pulled at him, a sense of a wisdom buried deep, a time long forgotten . . .

'Damien?'

He didn't move. He didn't even hear the call. He was caught for the moment in another time and place. The gardeners continued to rake the dead leaves around him, unwilling to interfere with the boy's thoughts as he stood transfixed before the fire.

In reality, he was standing in front of a large bonfire on the North Shore of Chicago, in the middle of a vast lawn that stretched almost as far as the eye could see in one direction and, at the other, came to an end before an enormous old mansion. This near-palace was the home of his aunt and uncle, who were now his foster parents.

But in his mind, he stood amid bright, continual flames, while all around him floated the sound of constant wailing and moaning – the cries of those who were suffering dreadfully, their pain made all the worse for knowing it would never end.

'DAMIEN!'

The vision fled. Damien Thorn shook his head and turned in the direction of the voice. He had to squint into the sun as it slowly set behind the gilded roof of his foster parents' summer home. High up on a third-

17

floor balcony, his cousin Mark was waving wildly to him.

Damien liked Mark. Mark was always kind, always generous, and he had made a genuine effort to welcome Damien into the fold seven years earlier. Now the two were closer than most twins ever were. Both were dressed in the neatly pressed uniforms of the military academy they attended. They had come home for the long Thanksgiving weekend, and now it was time to go back to school. Thanksgiving was always the saddest vacation of all, because it was then the Thorns closed up their summer home and moved into the city for the winter. So this was it, until next June.

Damien waved back to Mark. 'I'm coming!' he yelled, then turned to shake hands with the head gardener. 'See you next summer, Jim.' The old man had barely nodded his response when Damien took off with the grace and speed of a natural athlete, loping across the lawn and up to the massive front doors of the house.

As a sort of melancholy accompaniment, Mark pulled out his beloved bugle, leaned out over the balcony, and played 'Taps' into the darkening evening air.

Damien ran on toward the house, a young boy approaching his thirteenth birthday, the age when, as has been believed in most cultures for thousands of years, he would attain the full powers of manhood.

Reginald Thorn, Damien's grandfather on his late father's side, had discovered this plot of land on Lake Michigan, north of Chicago, in the 1920s. He had taken some of the money he had made in munitions in World War I to build a palace. People at the time had said he was crazy. It was not until years later, when automobiles, and politicians, had caused the Outer Drive to be built, that everyone who could afford to scrambled to build on the North Shore. But none of them ever built a home as fine as Thorn's.

Thorn used to say that he built the house for his sons, Robert and Richard. Those who envied Thorn, and who looked for every possible chance to slander or mock him, said that he had named his sons Robert and Richard so that they could all share the same monogrammed silverware, bath towels, and shirts. Thorn never denied the rumor, and it was certainly possible, for he was indeed miserly, as are many rich men who chase their way to the top. His haberdasher often had to wait more than a year for a Thorn bill to be honored, but he would never have considered refusing Thorn's business, for saying that you were Thorn's haberdasher was like having 'by appointment to His Majesty the King' posted on your window in Savile Row. Thorn was well aware of this, which was why he was rarely in a hurry to pay his bills.

Thorn adored both sons equally, and he did everything he could for them because they represented a kind of immortality to him. When they were refused admission to the exclusive Davidson Military School because their father was 'in trade,' Thorn donated enough money to build a new gym. The boys were admitted forthwith, the gym was named after their father, and both sons were graduated with honors.

It never occurred to Thorn that he might be hurting his boys by making life so easy for them. All he knew was that he wanted nothing less than the best for them. Always.

Robert, the elder, turned to international diplomacy. Richard went into the family business. Thorn was pleased with both. Everything was as it should be. With Robert making friends and waves in the world of politics, and Richard taking over Thorn Industries, their father had time to be lavish and self-indulgent. He established numerous grants, scholarships, and foundations, many of them connected with his grand passion, archaeology. Just before he died, he set in motion plans for the building of a great new museum in the heart of Chicago, a museum to be devoted primarily to the collecting and exhibiting of ancient Christian artifacts.

He did not live to see the museum completed. Nor did he live to see Thorn Industries become the most powerful conglomerate in the world.

Nor, fortunately, did he live to see his son, Robert, Ambassador to the Court of St. James, shot down at the height of his career, on the altar of a church, where he had apparently tried to murder his own young son, shortly after the tragic and inexplicable suicide of his beloved wife.

No one knew how much Damien remembered of that gray afternoon in London seven years earlier, when his father had dragged him, kicking and screaming, into a church in order to drive a cluster of daggers into his small, wildly beating heart – only to be stopped dead by a British constable's speeding bullet.

Although Damien seemed to remember nothing about it, the experience had obviously been traumatic, and Richard refused to allow any discussion of the topic. Richard's second wife, Ann, was a parlor child psychologist. She was convinced that the event was buried deep within Damien's subconscious and that it would only be a matter of time before the memory surfaced again, taking who knew what form of abnormal behaviour when it finally did. Richard would hear none of it when she expressed these fears to him. After all, didn't the boy have everything his heart desired?

Mark had been told nothing except that Damien's parents had both died in a terrible accident, and that the subject was so painful to Damien that he should never bring it up.

The only member of the family who was convinced that Damien remembered everything clearly and distinctly, as though it had happened the day before, was Marion Thorn. Aunt Marion, as everyone called her, was the sole surviving sibling of Reginald Thorn. She was a rare and strange old bird, disliked by all for her crotchety and stubborn ways, as well as for her tendency to meddle in other people's affairs. She had never married, having rejected all suitors on the grounds that they were after her money, and she had concentrated her attention on her nephews and their families. She had always preferred her nephew Robert, largely because he had left the family business in order to try something on his own. She had been devastated by the news of his sudden and tragic death, and she had never forgiven Damien for it. She *knew* that he was somehow responsible, although she did not know how or why.

The only reason anyone put up with her at all was that she controlled a substantial portion of Thorn Industries, which her brother Reginald had given her in a rare moment of irresponsible generosity. As a consequence, she had always been able to live quite comfortably, and had never become a live-in burden to any of her relatives. The fact that she controlled so much stock did not present much of a problem as long as she was alive, since she took no interest whatsoever in the running of the company. But when she did die, which might conceivably be soon, given the simple fact of her advanced age, she could cause a bit of a stir if she chose to do something unreasonable with her share of the business. She could, in fact, tip the whole balance of authority in the company if she so decided.

Aunt Marion knew she was not well liked, not that she minded. She'd never been popular. She was rarely invited to anyone's home for dinner, not even by her own relatives on the most traditional family holidays.

But this year, Aunt Marion had something very specific and very important to say, so she had swallowed her pride and her dignity and had invited herself to Richard Thorn's for the Thanksgiving weekend.

That Sunday night Aunt Marion watched as the boys said their good-byes in the front hall. The door was left wide open so that Murray, the chauffeur, had enough room to carry the boys' belongings out to the waiting limousine. It never failed – the boys always arrived with two bags and left with six. A burst of cold air blew through the front hall, and Richard Thorn, a handsome dark-haired man in his late fifties, stood off to one side and moved his arms in an effort to keep warm. He wanted to give his wife Ann some time to say good-bye to the boys. It hadn't been easy for her, marrying into a family as wealthy and tradition-bound as the Thorns. With great wealth, as with anything in excess, there were always complications. Neither of the boys was her own; Mark's mother, a lovely woman named Mary, who had been much closer in age to Richard than Ann was, had been killed suddenly in a freak car accident less than a year before Damien had come to live with Richard. For several months after the accident, Richard had been left to look after six-year-old Mark, and shortly thereafter Damien arrived. Richard's friends and family had been relieved to hear of his marriage to Ann; everyone understood that he needed someone to help raise the two boys. Ann was a bright, witty, attractive woman, full of energy and fun, and with an abundance of love and compassion for the tragedy-ridden family into which she had married. Damien took to her immediately; with Mark, it had taken a bit longer – but then he couldn't help comparing her to his mother, whom he had worshipped.

Now, seven years later, Ann stood in the doorway, hugging both boys at the same time, kissing their foreheads, making them promise to be good and to write, trying hard not to cry. Watching all this, Richard was

22

suddenly filled with renewed love for this remarkable woman who had come into his life at such a difficult and desperate time.

Mark broke away and ran up to Richard for a final hug. 'See you for our birthday, right, Dad?'

'You bet. Damien? Come here. Give your old man a hug, too.' Damien rushed over, although not quite so exuberantly. In the midst of a three-way hug, Murray appeared in the doorway and gave a discreet cough.

Ann laughed. 'We can take a hint, Murray,' she said, and moved toward Richard and the boys. Her men. 'Okay, guys, time to go.' After more hugs and kisses, the boys were finally ushered into the back seat of the sleek black car. Doors slammed, noses were pressed against the cold windowpanes for a last kiss good-bye, and then the car eased away, crunching gravel as it went down the driveway.

Richard and Ann stood together on the front steps and waved until the car rounded a bend and disappeared from sight.

As she and Richard turned to go back inside, Ann noticed that Aunt Marion was standing at her bedroom window on the second floor, also watching the boys' limousine fade away into the night. But as soon as Ann looked up, Aunt Marion pulled back, letting the curtain drop back into place.

Damien sank luxuriously into the back seat of the limousine. 'Oh, boy!' he exclaimed and let out a low whistle.

'You said it,' Mark agreed. 'What a weekend. I thought I was going to *scream*!'

'Well, let's do it now,' said Damien, and they both did, almost blasting Murray's eardrums.

'Murray,' said Damien, when the scream had subsided, 'give us a cigarette.'

Murray shook his head at the rearview mirror. 'You know the answer to that one, Damien.'

Damien shrugged. 'If you don't ask, you never know.' Suddenly he wheeled around in the seat, lifted his right hand to his face, and thumbed his nose in the direction of the house. 'Aunt Marion!' he shouted. 'For you!'

Mark joined in the salute with a loud and discordant note on his bugle. 'God,' he said, turning back, 'she's awful. Why do they ever let her *come*?'

'Just so she can wag her finger at us and criticize us and spoil our whole weekend, that's why,' Damien explained.

'At least we didn't have to have *another* dinner with her *tonight*.' Whenever Mark got overexcited about something, he tended to talk in italics. 'She's got to be a *hundred* years old,' he went on. 'And what's that *smell*?'

'That's lavender, you dope,' said Damien. 'All old ladies douse themselves in it.'

'Now, boys,' said Murray, interrupting their youthful cruelty, 'just because the woman's getting on –'

'Getting on our *nerves*!' said Mark, laughing at his own joke.

Damien's manner changed abruptly. 'Murray's right,' he said, much to his own amazement.

Mark looked at him to see if he was kidding. He wasn't.

'The poor woman's time is up,' Damien heard himself say. 'We shouldn't be making fun of her.'

Damien's manner was so odd that Mark fell silent. Murray finally broke the silence by changing the subject.

'Have you boys met your new platoon leader yet?' he asked.

They both shook their heads.

'I was hoping they wouldn't be able to *find* another one,' said Mark.

Damien shrugged. 'If you don't ask, you never know.' more like it.

'Did they ever tell you what happened to Sergeant Goodrich?' asked Murray.

'Nope,' said Damien, nudging Mark in the ribs with his elbow. Playtime again.

'They say he committed suicide.' Murray checked his rearview mirror for the boys' reaction. There was none. Suicide didn't seem to upset them.

'Well,' said Damien, 'when you've met one platoon leader, you've met them all.' And with that, he launched into a series of commands, barking them out as he simultaneously performed them with exaggerated perfection: 'Atten-*tion*! Eyes front! Ears back! Stomach in! *Butt out*!'

The boys collapsed with laughter. Mark looked at his cousin with affection. 'You're crazy, you know that?'

Damien nodded, then leaned over and whispered conspiratorially in his ear, 'I *practice*.'

Mark howled. 'And so do I!' He waved his bugle in the air.

'One more for Aunt Marion!' shouted Damien.

And Mark, ever eager to please his odd and wonderful foster brother, blew another loud, discordant note on his beloved bugle. But this one was clear and somehow chilling; it hung in the cold night air long after the car had disappeared into the vast darkness of the Illinois countryside.

The dining room table was large enough to seat twelve comfortably, but tonight there were only four. Richard Thorn sat at the head of the table with his wife, Ann, on his left. On his right was Aunt Marion, and on her right was a rumpled middle-aged man named Dr Charles Warren, who was curator of the Thorn Museum and one of the world's great authorities on ancient Christian artifacts.

25

The butler, who had just entered to ask if anyone wanted more coffee, caught Richard's expression and retired the instant he read the signal. Aunt Marion was preparing herself – and everyone else within earshot – for one of her rampages, and Richard didn't want the help overhearing any more than they already had.

'It's late, and I'm tired,' Aunt Marion began, turning her gaze on the other three at the table to make sure that all eyes were clearly focused on her. 'I shall get to the point. I'm getting old and I'm going to die soon.' She looked directly at Ann. 'Save your sighs of relief for later.' Ann tried to protest, but Aunt Marion went on. 'I own twenty-seven percent of Thorn Industries, and I have the right to dispose of my share any way I see fit.'

'We know that,' said Richard, as he did whenever Aunt Marion brought up the matter.

'You also know,' continued Marion, 'that, at the moment, I've left everything to you, Richard.'

He nodded. 'Go on.'

'I'm here to tell you tonight,' she said, 'that unless you do what I ask –'

Thorn threw down his napkin. He could not countenance anything that even remotely approached blackmail. 'Don't threaten me, Marion,' he warned, his blood pressure rising. 'I'm not concerned about –'

'You can't be *un*concerned,' she interrupted, 'about a sum that's close to three billion dollars! '

Dr Warren stood up, obviously embarrassed by the discussion. 'I really don't see why I should be here,' he said, and made a move to leave.

Aunt Marion stopped him. 'You're here, Dr Warren, because you're curator of the Thorn Museum. And I also happen to own twenty-seven percent of *that*! '

Warren sat back down.

Aunt Marion was having a marvellous time. She had everyone's complete and undivided attention. She could feel Ann's piercing gaze upon her, but knowing already that Ann loathed her, she didn't care. She had never liked Ann either. She'd always had a feeling that Ann's timing in entering Richard's life was *too* perfect, that there was an element of the fortune-hunter about her, and that the persistence with which she'd gone after Richard so soon after the death of his first wife was not unlike a buzzard's circling a brand-new corpse.

But Aunt Marion shook that thought from her mind. She had something else to say tonight. She leaned forward in her chair and said, very slowly and very distinctly, 'I want you to take the boys out of the military academy and to put them in separate schools.'

There was a long silence, and finally Ann said with equal poise and deliberation, 'Where the boys are concerned, I don't care what you want. They're not your sons, they're ours.'

Which is exactly what Marion hoped she would say. 'May I remind you,' she said with a small smile, 'that neither boy is *yours*. Mark is Richard's son by his first wife, and Damien is his brother's son!'

Ann trembled with rage. It was all she could do to keep the tears from starting up. She pushed back her chair and stood up. 'Thank you,' she snapped. 'Thank you very much!'

Richard took her arm gently and eased her back down into her seat. Then he turned to Marion. 'What's all this about, for God's sake?'

'Get Mark away from Damien,' said the old woman, her eyes afire with conviction. 'They don't belong together. Damien's a terrible influence; can't you see it? Do you want to ruin Mark, *destroy him*?'

Richard jumped to his feet. 'That's it,' he said. 'I'll see you up to your room, Marion.'

Aunt Marion stood up to face him. 'You're blind, Richard, purposely blind!' She took hold of both his hands. 'You know your brother tried to kill Damien –'

Dr Warren looked shocked. This was news to him.

Ann jumped up again and shouted, 'Get her out of here, Richard! Get her *out*!'

Aunt Marion knew it was now or never. She kept right on going. 'Why did he try to kill Damien? Answer me! Tell the *truth*!'

Richard could barely control his rage. 'Robert was *ill*,' he said through tightly clenched teeth, 'mentally –'

'Stop it!' cried Ann. 'Don't even *talk* to her!'

Dr Warren didn't know what to do. He was both embarrassed and fascinated. He sat there very quietly, twisting his napkin in his hands and trying to act invisible.

Aunt Marion took one more deep breath and made a final effort, but now she was pleading. 'If you don't send Damien away, I am going to leave everything I own to a charity, any charity –'

'Do what you want!' bellowed Richard. 'Burn the money, throw it away, but just don't try to –'

'Richard, please!' begged Marion. 'Listen to me!' She was starting to cry. 'You know what I'm saying is true. I may be old, but I'm not insane. Your brother tried to *kill* Damien. WHY?!'

'Get out!' Ann screamed. She started around the table as though she were actually going to strike the old woman. Richard stopped her, but she shook herself loose from his grasp and pointed with a trembling finger. 'Tell-her-to-*go*!'

'I'm going!' said Aunt Marion, and mustering all her dignity, she nodded good night to Dr Warren and left the room. Richard followed right behind her.

When their footsteps had receded into the echoing distance of the huge house, Ann turned to Dr Warren and let out an enormous sigh. 'I'm so sorry, Charles,' she apologized. 'I had no *idea* –'

'No, it's all right,' Warren assured her. 'I understand.' He rose and headed for the den. 'Why don't we go set up the slides?' he asked, changing the subject. 'I have some wonderful things I want to show you and Richard.'

What he really wanted was simply to be out of that room.

By the time they had reached the second-floor landing, Aunt Marion had succeeded in wrenching her arm away from Richard's grasp. 'I can walk by myself!' she said stiffly. They walked in silence down the long, carpeted corridor, but when they reached her bedroom door, she turned around to face him. 'Your brother tried to kill Damien –'

'We've been through this, Aunt Marion.'

'There must have been a *reason*.'

'I've told you before. I don't like to talk about it. Especially not in front of guests! Jesus Christ –'

'But why would he try to kill his own son?'

'He was *ill*, Aunt Marion, emotionally and mentally ill.'

'And what about Damien? You think he's not?'

'There is nothing wrong with Damien!' Thorn found himself shouting again. It infuriated him that she could enrage him so easily. Perhaps she would let up if he reacted less vehemently. He tried to calm down, tried to sound reasonable. 'You've built up this hatred of him based on absolutely nothing.'

'Look carefully,' advised Aunt Marion.

It's finally happened, Thorn thought. She's finally gone round the bend. 'Go to bed. Please,' he said. 'You're not in control of yourself right now.'

Aunt Marion raised an eyebrow. She knew how to strike him where it hurt. She'd remind him just how much in control she was. 'Damien will inherit nothing from me. I'll see to that tomorrow!' She reached for the doorknob.

Thorn grabbed her hand. 'Do what you want; the shares in the company are yours.' He knew he sounded desperate. He needed those shares to protect the interests of his two sons. 'But when you're in *my* house –'

'I'm *your* guest,' she finished the sentence for him. 'I know. But this is *my* room, and I'll have to ask you to leave. Now.'

Thorn sighed and rubbed his hand over his forehead. He was usually so calm, even under the most difficult of circumstances. But this one old woman could really get to him. He leaned down and gave her a swift kiss on the top of her head. 'Murray will have the car ready for you in the morning.' Then he turned to join the others downstairs.

Aunt Marion waited until he had disappeared into the shadows at the end of the corridor before she broke into a triumphant smile; she marched into her room, slamming the door behind her.

By the time Richard joined Ann and Dr Warren in the den, they had already set up the slide projector and a screen so that Charles could give them a preliminary glimpse of the new exhibition he was bringing to the Thorn Museum in Chicago.

Thorn had inherited a love of archaeology from his father, and had continued to support the undertakings Reginald Thorn had begun in that field. One such venture had been a risky dig outside the small town of Acre, which produced the most startling find of the last twenty years. Although it was Reginald Thorn who had been responsible for initiating the excavation, it was Richard who was to reap its rewards.

He dimmed the light as Charles Warren set the projector in motion. 'A good many of these things have already been packed and sent on their way,' Charles said. 'We should have the first shipment shortly.'

The first few slides were of vases and small statues. Looking at them, Thorn seemed to forget all about

30

Aunt Marion. Ann looked over at her husband and smiled. His enthusiasm and the intensity with which he responded to the few people and things that he cherished had had a lot to do with her marrying him.

Charles interrupted Ann's musing. 'Here's something that'll interest you,' he said. She looked back at the screen and gasped involuntarily. The slide was of a fairly large statue, hideously detailed and in vivid color; it showed a licentious woman, clothed in purple, scarlet, and gold, wearing many jewels, triumphantly astride a seven-headed Beast. Each head was attached to a long, scaly neck, and had horns and fangs and a thin, forked tongue. The woman's head was thrown back, her long hair wild and twisted, and she seemed drunk with the contents of the golden cup held in her hand.

'Oh, dear,' Ann murmured.

'Yes,' said Charles, 'she is a bit frightening.'

'The Whore of Babylon?' asked Richard.

Charles nodded. Ann looked askance at her husband. 'You *know* her?' she asked, and everyone laughed. Charles found a pencil and walked up to the screen. 'She represents Rome,' he said, 'and these ten razor-sharp horns on the Beast are the ten kings who have no kingdoms yet, but who have been promised temporary power by Satan until he makes his grand appearance.'

'Why is she riding the Beast?' asked Ann.

'I don't know,' said Charles, 'but apparently she didn't stay on for long. According to the Book of Revelation, the ten kings "shall hate the whore and shall make her desolate and naked, and shall eat her flesh, and burn her with fire." '

'Terrific,' said Ann, shuddering. 'Do you believe all that stuff?'

'Well, what I guess I believe is that the Bible is composed of grand and wonderful metaphors. It's up to us to find meanings that are useful to us.'

'Like what, for instance?' Ann was intrigued.

Charles seemed hesitant. He wasn't one to proselytize. And it hadn't been so long ago that he, too, had scoffed at any sort of religious faith. His interest in things religious had merely been scholarly. But then, slowly, gradually, the sense that there *was* a God, and a pattern to things, and a reason behind it all, had begun to seep into his consciousness. There was such a consistency to the ancient artifacts he had uncovered – no matter where the dig, or what the date of the art – there was such similarity that it had to be more than coincidence. And then, once he had accepted the possibility that there was a God, everything had changed – his work, the way he perceived things, his relationships with other people.

Charles decided to go ahead and answer Ann's question honestly. 'Well,' he began slowly, 'there is a great deal of evidence that the end of the world may be near.'

'What?' Ann thought he was joking.

'A great many things that have happened in the last decade were prophesied in the Book of Revelation,' he said. 'Earthquakes, floods, famine, the sky darkening over with smog, the waters becoming polluted, climates changing . . .'

'But those things have always gone on,' Ann protested.

'There are more specific things as well. For example, there's the prophecy that the end of the world would come shortly after the Bible had been translated into every written language. That just happened in the early sixties. And there's another prophecy that the final holocaust would be generated in the Middle East.'

'But –' Ann began.

Richard interrupted. 'Do you mind if we get back to the slides? If the end is so near, I'm anxious to see what else I've paid for, before it's all blown to smithereens!'

The tension was broken. Even Charles had to laugh.

He pushed the remote control button. The next slide was also of the Whore, but taken from a greater distance, and with a young woman standing next to it to give some idea of the size of the statue.

'Who's the girl?' asked Richard.

'Phew!' said Ann. 'I thought you were going to identify her, too!'

'A friend of mine,' said Charles. 'A journalist. Her name's Joan Hart. Have you heard of her? She's doing a biography of Bugenhagen, the archaeologist.'

The next slide was a close-up of Joan: a striking-looking woman, with auburn hair and flashing eyes.

'You seem taken with her, Charles,' Ann said.

Charles shook his head and laughed. 'Not by a long shot. But she's very good at what she does. As a matter of fact, she's coming to Chicago. Soon, I think. She wants to interview you, Richard.'

'Me?' asked Richard. 'What for?'

'Background on the dig, the exhibition,' said Charles. 'That sort of thing.'

'You know I hate to give interviews, Charles.'

'I know.'

'Of *any* kind.'

'I know, but I thought –'

'Tell her that.'

'All right, all right.' Charles shook his head at Richard's reluctance to be interviewed, although he knew that Thorn had always insisted on privacy, on a life away from the public eye, and he had to admit he respected that. He wasn't sure he could be so disciplined were he as much in the limelight as Thorn was. But maybe that's why Thorn was in the limelight and he was not. God worked in mysterious ways, after all.

A short while later, the three of them were standing in the front hall saying good night.

'I'll be in town tomorrow,' said Richard, helping Charles on with his coat, 'but Ann has to stay here to close the house.'

Charles nodded. 'It's been a good summer,' he said and turned to kiss Ann.

'I'll see you the day after tomorrow,' she said, opening the front door. 'Drive carefully.'

Richard walked Charles to his car. 'About Aunt Marion –' he began.

'Already forgotten,' smiled Charles as he slid behind the wheel. Richard closed the door and stood back to wave good-bye as Charles drove off in to the cold November night. Then he exhaled a big puff of frosty breath and headed back inside.

Unknown to those below, Aunt Marion had heard every word of the parting conversation, including Richard's attempt to apologize for her behavior that evening. She had opened her window before getting into bed, as she did every night. She claimed that the cold night air did her good.

Tonight, however, the open window also served to allow her to overhear Richard's apology, which she found totally unnecessary. 'Ungrateful wretch,' she muttered to herself. She returned her attention to the well-worn Bible which she read every night before going to sleep. This evening she turned to Genesis 1: 28:

Be fruitful, and multiply, and replenish the earth and subdue it: and have dominion over the fish of the sea, and over the fowl of the air, and over every living thing that moveth upon the earth.

'Well,' she mused, 'if *that* isn't a sign I don't know what *is*!' She interpreted the passage to refer to Thorn Industries, that the company was destined for far greater things than anyone imagined, and she was more determined than ever that her shares should not fall into the hands of that evil little Damien. She decided to change her will as soon as she returned home the next day. She would give the shares to some well-intentioned religious group. *That* would show them all!

So absorbed was she in her fantasy of revenge that she failed to notice the enormous black raven that had settled lightly on her windowsill, regarding her solemnly with malevolent eyes . . .

Richard was reading in bed. He wore an old-fashioned pair of glasses and was surrounded by mounds of company reports. He often used the late-night hours to try to keep abreast of things. Even so, he never seemed to be able to catch up on everything that was going on at Thorn Industries. There was so much to keep track of, and things were constantly changing.

But tonight he found he was having trouble concentrating. Aunt Marion's tactless reference to his brother's death had upset him. A whole rush of memories had been resurrected and were swirling about in his mind, memories that were better left buried. Who knew what his brother might have become? Perhaps even President. But to have been shot down in the prime of his life like some mad dog . . .

'*Richard*!' Ann, sitting at her dressing table, stopped in mid-stroke of brushing her hair. She had obviously been trying to get his attention for some time. He pushed his glasses up onto his forehead and looked over at her.

'I asked you to promise me,' she said.

'Promise you what, honey?'

Ann sighed. It was clear he hadn't heard a word she had said. 'That we'll never have Aunt Marion here again. Ever.'

'Oh, Ann –'

'Promise me!'

35

'The woman's eighty-four years old, for Chrissake!'

'I don't care. I don't like having her around. She's evil and she's dangerous and –'

'She's *senile*, Ann.'

'She pollutes the air with her senility, then. She upsets me, and she frightens the boys –'

'Nonsense. They think she's funny.'

'No. They make fun *of* her, but they can't stand to be in the same room with her. Especially Damien.'

Richard removed his glasses and put then on the bedside table. It was obvious that he would get no more reading done tonight. He gathered up all the reports and put them on the floor. 'Well,' he said, trying to lighten the conversation, 'at least she only opens her mouth once every few years, like someone running for reelection.'

'Not funny,' said Ann. She put down her hairbrush and turned off the dressing table light. Then she stood up, stretched, and walked over to the bed. Richard was always amazed at how beautiful she was, and how lucky he was to have found her when he did. After Mary died so suddenly and horribly, he felt sure that he would never again be in love. And then Ann came, like a gift from God. They had met briefly in Washington. He had been there on business, and she had just moved there to start a new career, working for HEW. At first, she had flirted with him outrageously until he told her about Mary's death and his reluctance to embark on a new involvement. She had become very thoughtful then, very sympathetic. Perhaps nothing would have come of it had he not found her sitting next to him in first-class on his flight back to Chicago. She had insisted that it was coincidence, and he had allowed her that, but he was flattered nonetheless, and intrigued. Their courtship was brief and intense, and their engagement announcement came as a great surprise to the outside world. But Richard was beyond worrying about social considerations at that point; not only was he too important to be threatened by gossip, but, more to the point, by then he was also wildly, madly, in love with Ann.

And here she was, seven years later, in his arms, and he was still obsessed with her. Sex had a lot to do with it, he had to admit. Ann had taken him to heights that seemed all but sinful. Mary had been almost shy in bed, whereas Ann was aggressive, seductive, addicting. Richard could hardly believe how much sexuality had been lying dormant in him, unaroused until Ann came into his life.

'What are you thinking?' Ann broke into his reverie.

'About you. How we met. How much I love you.'

'Oh, *that*.'

He laughed. That was another thing. Ann could make him laugh in ways he had never laughed with Mary. But he resisted comparing the two. It made him feel guilty.

'Feeling guilty again?' she asked. She had a way of reading his mind as well.

'No,' he lied. He didn't feel like getting into that old routine again tonight. Too many other things were on his mind. It had been a charged evening without adding to it.

Ann nuzzled up against him. 'What did you say to her?' she purred into his neck.

'Hmmm?'

'What did you say to Aunt Marion when you took her upstairs?'

'I told her to behave herself.'

'That's all?' She began pressing up against him.

'Well, I was a little firmer than that.'

'Firmer than this?' Richard loved how sexy she made him feel. He wrapped his legs around her and drew her in as close as was physically possible. This was one woman he did *not* want to lose. One loss was enough.

Hadn't he had enough death by now? If there was a God, wouldn't He judge that Richard Thorn had had enough sorrow in his life?

He was happy now, finally. So happy, in fact, that he allowed himself to fantasize that things would stay forever just as they were. With Ann, and Mark, and Damien. With Ann, it had been virtually love at first sight, and it had stayed that way so far. So far, so good. He had loved Mark at first sight, too. He hadn't been able to get to the hospital for the birth – it had happened so swiftly and prematurely – but he did see his first, and only, son when he was but a few hours old. Tiny and new and sleeping soundly against his mother's breast. Richard's love for and pride in Mark had increased with the years.

With Damien, it had been more difficult. For a long time, Damien had reminded Richard of his dead brother, and he almost resented the child for that. But as the years went by, he came to love Damien as his own son and to take pride in the boy's accomplishments and growth.

'Damien's such a good kid,' murmured Ann, seeming to read his mind again. 'Why does Aunt Marion hate him so much?'

'Don't know, honey,' he replied.

'She upset you, too, didn't she?'

'The evening wasn't exactly a social triumph.'

'I don't mean that,' said Ann, rising herself up on one elbow. With her free hand, she gently traced the outline of his face. 'She stirs up all your old memories of your brother, doesn't she?'

Richard tensed. There were some things he revealed to no one, not even his wife. 'I'd rather not talk about it.'

Ann let it pass. She probed because she cared, but she knew when to stop. Her eyes suddenly took on a mischievous twinkle. 'Maybe if she'd gotten married, she wouldn't be such an old witch.' She slid back down against him.

'Amazing what a good man can do,' said Richard, as he moved to get even closer.

She held him off for just one more second. 'Promise?' she asked with that little-girl look in her eyes that he found he was unable to resist.

'I promise,' he said, reaching to turn off the light. 'No more Aunt Marion.'

Two other lights went out at that same moment. The light in Aunt Marion's room, and the light in Aunt Marion's eyes.

The old woman was dead, her Bible fallen from her hands.

No one knew, no one except the huge black raven which flew out of her bedroom and circled away into the night.

CHAPTER TWO

Very early the next morning, the entire Davidson Military Academy was out on the parade ground in full regalia, marching to the beat of the loud and brassy school band which brought up the rear.

Most of the cadets were struggling to wake up, hoping they remembered enough about the maneuvers to execute them at the crack of dawn with at least a semblance of military proficiency.

The cadets were finally in position for a special assembly; sectioned off, platoon by platoon. The band came to a halt, marched in place for the last measure of the music, then stopped. The last note echoed in the cold autumnal air.

The Colonel stood on the wide steps leading up to the main school building and smiled with pride at the rows of young cadets in perfect formation below him. He was much too fat for a military man, but since he knew he would never again be asked to fight for his country, he had let his body go, giving way to one of the minor pleasures in life.

Beside him stood a handsome, alert, stern-looking young man, whose lean, taut muscles rippled like water under his neatly pressed uniform. His physical condition was a walking rebuke to the Colonel.

The Colonel began by welcoming the boys back from Thanksgiving vacation. Then he launched into a series of general remarks about the schedule for the weeks to come.

Down below on the parade ground, Mark whispered

to Damien out of the side of his mouth, 'That must be him.' He was referring to the young career soldier standing next to the Colonel.

'He looks okay,' Damien whispered back.

'If you like gorillas.'

Just then, the Colonel concluded his brief announcements with: 'Bradley Platoon, hold fast. All other platoons to the canteen. By the right flank . . . MARCH!'

The band started up again and played until everyone was off the field except the two dozen cadets in Mark and Damien's platoon.

'At ease,' said the Colonel.

The boys shifted as a unit. The Colonel nodded in the direction of the young man at his side. 'This is Sergeant Daniel Neff. He's taking over as Platoon Officer from Sergeant Goodrich.'

This was the first mention of Sergeant Goodrich. Death was never spoken of to cadets when it was at all possible to avoid the subject – a peculiar irony for a military academy – and the topic of suicide was especially avoided, since the act was considered unmanly and unheroic. So the late Sergeant Goodrich would not be referred to again.

'Sergeant Neff is a very experienced soldier,' the Colonel went on, 'and I'm sure before many weeks you'll be the smartest platoon in the Academy.' The Colonel attempted a friendly smile. Then he turned to Neff. 'I'll leave any further introductions to you, Sergeant.'

Neff saluted smartly and watched as the Colonel waddled off, attempting to pull his unsuitable body into something approaching a military posture.

In the back row of the platoon stood an ungainly hulk of a boy, a full head taller than any of the others. He was startlingly obese for such a young man, and his neck and wrists protruded like ugly bulbs from a shirt

41

that was too tight for him. His name was Teddy, and he compensated for his unpleasant appearance by bullying the other cadets, all of whom were smaller than he. Teddy's specialty, under the guise of fun, was a paralyzing punch to the shoulder that left its recipient's arm deadened for nearly twenty minutes.

Teddy decided it would be a good idea to play up to the new platoon leader at the outset, to be the first one to make an impression. He looked at the gleaming array of metal on Neff's chest. 'Sergeant,' he said, smiling obsequiously, 'what are your medals –'

'You'll speak to me only when you're spoken to,' barked Neff, 'and you'll listen to every word I say! Because I intend to *shine* in my new job, and the only way I can shine is by making *you* shine. You're the little unit I have to polish until the glare of your achievement blinds everybody on this parade ground!'

Neff paused and swept them all with his glance. '*Understood*?'

The platoon, much paler than before Neff had begun speaking, nodded their heads quietly, instantly in awe of their new leader. Teddy lowered his head and swallowed hard. He didn't like having been shamed before his peers. He'd have to get even, somehow.

'I'll meet each of you personally in my office after breakfast,' Neff said. 'But for now, let's have your names.' He stood in front of Mark.

'Mark Thorn,' said Mark, quivering under Neff's stare.

'I like my rank, Thorn.'

'Mark Thorn, *Sergeant*!'

'Thorn, heh?' said Neff, smiling. 'Your family's got strong connections with this place, hasn't it?'

Mark, who, having been born to wealth and power, had been taught that it was rude to remind other people of that fact, didn't know what to say. So he said nothing, which didn't satisfy Neff.

42

'Well, hasn't it?'

Mark decided on a diplomatically noncommittal answer. 'My father and uncle were cadets here.'

'Good,' said Neff, impressed by Mark's presence of mind under the circumstances. 'But understand,' he went on, 'that doesn't entitle you to privileges. We're all the same here.'

Mark nodded sharply, anxious for Neff to move on. 'Yes, Sergeant!'

Teddy couldn't resist the chance to redeem himself. 'We've all heard *that* line before,' he said in a stage whisper. The cadets around him froze.

Neff whirled on Teddy and pointed angrily, 'But not from me, you haven't!'

This new guy meant business. Teddy could not hold up under Neff's hard stare. Again, he lowered his eyes, and again, he felt humiliated.

Neff moved on down the line. 'Name?' he asked.

'Damien Thorn . . . Sergeant.'

Neff shot a quick glance at Mark, then looked back at Damien. 'You don't look alike,' he said.

'Cousins, Sergeant,' said Damien, taking a risk and flashing a brilliant smile.

There was a flicker of something in Neff's eyes, but it was gone as quickly as it had appeared. 'All right,' he said. 'But the same goes for you. No privileges.'

Damien nodded, and followed Neff with his eyes as the Sergeant moved on to the next cadet. There was something about this man that unnerved Damien, that made him feel oddly excited. But exactly what it was, he was unable to tell. At least, not yet.

Sixty miles away, in the heart of Chicago, Richard Thorn walked across the ornate lobby of the enormous building that was the home office of Thorn Industries. With him was Bill Atherton, president of the company. There were a few other people about, but for the most part, it was still too early for any but the most diligent workaholics, or those just coming off the night shift.

Atherton, the kindest and most self-effacing of men, would have made a superb spy. No one ever noticed him. At sixty-four, he glided through life as if on one of those moving walkways in airports, getting slowly but surely to his destination with no discernible effort.

Upon graduation from college, Atherton had gone to work for Thorn Industries in Planning and Development. He had gradually worked his way up the corporate ladder until he was now second only to Richard Thorn, who was the chairman of the board and chief executive officer. He still lived in the house he had bought when he married his college sweetheart. She was still his wife, still his sweetheart, and the first and only woman with whom he had ever been to bed. Life held no surprises for Bill Atherton, and he was vaguely puzzled by the ups and downs of friends whose existences were far more volatile than his own.

Atherton may have been a bit bland, but he was far from stupid. No one got to be president of Thorn Industries by being stupid. Today he had something specific on his mind, something that had been bothering him for quite a while now. It had to do with Paul Buher, director of Special Projects and Atherton's immediate subordinate.

A young man, nearly thirty years younger than Atherton, Buher had made no secret of the fact that he wanted Atherton's job. But that wasn't what bothered Atherton. He was immune to company politics. He had kept his job by doing his work well, and he knew that Richard Thorn, who was one of his oldest and dearest friends, was not the kind of man to be swayed by any Machiavellian maneuverings. What bothered Atherton was that the more he got to know Buher, the more he found him ruthless and unprincipled. Buher's way of operating was bad for the company image, and, what

44

was even more important, it was likely to get Thorn Industries into serious trouble, particularly if Buher was given any more responsibility than he already had.

All of this was running through Atherton's mind as he crossed the lobby with Richard Thorn and headed for the revolving doors. They were on their way to a meeting scheduled by Buher to check out a special, agriculturally – oriented plant that Buher wanted Thorn Industries to buy.

Atherton had made a point of getting to work early enough that morning so that he could share some of his thoughts about Buher with Thorn *before* they got to the plant. Once they got there, he knew he'd have no chance.

Thorn was his usual diplomatic self. 'I'm the first to admit Paul's difficult to get along with,' he said, as the two men reached the revolving doors, 'but it took us three years to find a man with his qualifications.'

'I'm not questioning his qualifications,' Atherton said. 'It's –'

'– his manner.' Thorn finished the sentence for him as they moved through the doors and out onto the sidewalk. The limousine was there, waiting for them.

Atherton shook his head in disagreement. 'I can even cope with his manner,' he said. 'I've met and dealt with every kind in my day. No. I don't like what he's proposing. It sticks in my craw, and I don't intend to hide my feelings.'

'You're worried that it could make trouble for us with the Justice Department,' Thorn said.

'Well, he's dealing with some very touchy issues . . .'

As they approached the limousine, Murray got out and opened the door for them.

'Let's hear him out,' Thorn said as they climbed into the back seat. 'All I'm asking is that you couch your objections a little more . . . delicately . . . than usual.'

45

Murray closed the door on Atherton's appreciative laugh.

At the Academy, the Bradley Platoon was in the process of meeting their new leader, one by one. They stood quietly in the corridor outside his office, anxiously awaiting their turn to be called in.

Teddy lounged against one wall, affecting an air of supreme boredom. It was very important to him that he appear totally unafraid of this man who had humiliated him, not once but twice, before the other cadets.

Teddy was, in fact, already very much afraid of Neff, who obviously was neither impressed nor amused by brash outspokenness on the part of any of the cadets. Teddy was going to have to figure a way around him, or change his act altogether.

As usual, a few sycophants were gathered around Teddy, imitating his attitude of indifference. Restless with anticipation, Teddy suddenly decided to start a little action. He walked over to the opposite wall where perhaps forty framed photographs hung neatly in rows. They were pictures of all the Academy football teams, arranged chronologically. It was fascinating to study them in order; one could learn not only about the way the game of football had evolved over the years, but also something about the kind of young men who used to attend the school as contrasted with the kind who were enrolled now. Perhaps the simplest way to describe the change would be to say that where there once was a kind of uniform pride, there now was an unifying attitude of anger or resentment.

Teddy finally found what he was looking for. 'My old man played on this team,' he said. 'That's him.' He pointed with a stubby finger. Half a dozen hangers-on moved in to look. 'He was on the line,' he said, pausing to look over at Damien. 'Robert Thorn played quarterback.' There was obvious disdain in his voice. 'I guess you can *buy* anything.'

Damien pushed away from the wall where he'd been leaning. 'Teddy,' he said, not bothering to disguise the threat in his voice.

Teddy looked around at his fan club. They were clearly eager for more. He decided to go for the punch line: 'Did he ever get his "quarter" back?'

There were nervous chuckles all around. Just as Damien was about to go for Teddy, the door to Neff's office suddenly swung open and Mark stepped out. He immediately sensed the tension in the air and noticed the hostility focused between his cousin and Teddy. He cleared his throat and said calmly, 'Damien – you're next.'

Damien looked first at Mark, then back at Teddy. 'Don't you ever,' he said, with surprising menace in his manner and his tone, 'mention my father's name in my presence again. *Ever*.' And with that, he turned smartly and disappeared into Neff's office, closing the door gently behind him.

Teddy looked at Mark and snorted. 'Your cousin really thinks he's "somebody," doesn't he?' He turned to his audience. 'My father says the Thorns have to have their hats specially made because no store sells hats large enough for their big heads!' Teddy burst into a nasty laugh, and most of the cadets followed suit, afraid not to.

Mark walked up to Teddy very calmly and asked him brightly, 'Are you a philatelist?'

Teddy wasn't sure what that meant, though he suspected it was an insult. Moreover, he couldn't believe that Mark Thorn was actually taking him on. Damien, sure; he was the tough one. But Mark?

'Am I a what?' asked Teddy, pulling himself up tall so that he towered over Mark even more.

47

'Let me rephrase it,' said Mark, remaining amazingly calm under the circumstances. 'Do you collect stamps?'

'No,' said Teddy, wondering what the hell Mark was up to.

'Well,' said Mark, grinning, 'you're about to start. *Now*!' And with that, he stamped down hard on Teddy's left foot.

Teddy was stunned. Absolutely immobilized. Not so much by the fact that this punk kid had stamped on his foot, although that had him stifling a yell and hopping about on one leg, but that he had dared to do it. No one at the Academy had ever defied him like that before, let alone done physical damage to him; Teddy simply didn't know what to make of it.

Never too mentally swift at best, he was still trying to figure out what to make of this startling development when Mark, shaking his head in mock sadness, brought his heel down on his other foot! Now Teddy was not only bewildered, he was also unable to stand.

The other cadets were tempted to laugh, since Teddy looked so ludicrous hopping from one foot to the other. But they knew a big fight was coming, and they knew who'd come out on top, so they figured they had better honor their original allegiance and refrain from laughing. Instead, they backed away to leave Mark alone with Teddy.

Damien stood at perfect military ease before the large desk, behind which sat Neff, riffling through Damien's file. Finally Neff found what he was looking for. He ran his finger down a list of grades.

'Mathematics,' he began, 'good. Science . . . very good. Military history . . . fair.' He raised an eyebrow. 'Room for improvement.'

'Yes, Sergeant.' Damien was barely paying attention. He was rocking ever so imperceptibly back and forth on his heels, and watching out the window behind Neff

48

as the youngest of the Academy's platoons ran outside for their morning recess.

'Physical training,' continued Neff, 'excellent.' He pushed the file aside and leaned forward, clasping his hands together. 'I hear you're quite a football player.'

Damien shrugged. He knew he was good but saw no point in boasting about it. Words meant nothing. Actions were all.

'Be *proud* of your accomplishments!' barked Neff, startling Damien into standing still. 'Pride's all right when there's reason to be proud!' He pounded his fist on the desk for emphasis.

'Yes, Sergeant.' He didn't know what else to say.

Neff leaned back in his chair. 'I'll be watching the game this afternoon,' he said. It sounded more like a challenge than a simple statement. Damien nodded. Neff was beginning to disturb him.

There was an awkward silence as Neff seemed to gather his thoughts. Finally, he closed his eyes and spoke with great emotion.

'I'm here to teach you,' he said quietly, 'but I'm also here to . . . help you.' He seemed to be struggling to find the right words. 'Any problems, come to me. Don't be afraid –'

'Afraid?' thought Damien. He was paying attention now.

'– Day or night, any advice . . . come to me.' Neff opened his eyes. 'Do you understand?'

Damien didn't, but he nodded anyway. 'Yes, Sergeant.' It sounded convincing.

'We're going to get to know each other,' Neff went on. Then he looked back at the file and tapped a particular paragraph. 'I see you're an orphan.'

Damien nodded uncomfortably.

Neff smiled sympathetically. 'So am I,' he said. 'That's something we have in common.'

Damien looked at Neff strangely. Something was

going on at this meeting that he didn't entirely understand, and he didn't like it.

Neff's smile suddenly disappeared, he stood up and whirled around to face out the window. Once more his voice was cold and formal. He wiped his brow, and then said, by way of dismissal, 'Send Foster in.'

Damien stared at his back for a second, then turned and slipped out.

When Neff heard the door close behind him, he dropped his head onto his chest and let out a deep breath, as though he had just barely made it through something that was not only extremely important but extremely difficult as well.

Damien stepped out into the corridor in time to see Teddy deliver what was clearly the final blow to poor Mark, who was squirming on the ground, trying to protect his already battered face.

Damien didn't even stop to think. '*TEDDY*!' It was a voice unlike any Damien had ever used before, unlike any that the boys in the hallway had ever heard. It had a depth and a resonance that was terrifying, and a level of command that was irresistible.

Teddy turned around, grinning triumphantly. But as he stared into Damien's cold and penetrating eyes, his grin began to fade.

The other cadets fell silent.

And then came the sound, a clattering, like thin metal rulers being clapped together. Teddy looked around for the source of the noise. No one else seemed to hear it. They were all staring at him. The clattering grew louder until it became clear that it was the sound of large, powerful *wings* beating in the air – just above Teddy's head! He whirled around, shrieking 'Stop it!' and flailing his arms at something invisible that was attacking his head.

The other cadets stared, open-mouthed. Damien

seemed to be in a trance. Mark struggled to his feet to see what was happening.

Finally, Teddy was lifted up off the ground, as if caught in some kind of wind current, and flung against the wall!

Just then, the door to Neff's office flew open and Neff stepped out into the hallway. The sudden interruption broke Damien's trance; he shook his head free and blinked his eyes. Teddy sat slumped in the corner. The sound had subsided. The other cadets stood absolutely still.

'What are you doing on the floor?' Neff asked Teddy.

Teddy said nothing. He just sat there, whimpering and rubbing his jaw.

'Who hit you?' Neff persisted.

Teddy struggled to stand up. 'Nobody, sir.' It wasn't exactly a lie.

Neff seemed to accept that. 'Okay,' he said. 'Foster next.' He turned and walked back into his office. The cadet named Foster folowed him in, closing the door quietly behind him.

The silence that ensued was unbearable. Finally Damien pushed his way through the cadets who were now crowding around Teddy, and made his way outside. Mark was close on his heels.

Halfway down the wide outdoor steps, Mark caught up with Damien. 'What did you *do* to him?' he asked, genuinely concerned.

'I don't know,' said Damien. He meant it. He had hardly known what was happening or who was responsible for it. Maybe he was going crazy, too, like his father.

Mark put his arm around him, and they walked this way for a while. Finally, Mark said, 'They've asked me to join the band.'

Damien smiled, glad for the change of subject. 'Hey,' he said, 'that's great! ' He almost seemed to be himself

51

again – carefree, funny, charismatic. He had a twinkle in his eye as he nudged Mark gently. 'Once around the field,' he said, pushing Mark in front of him. 'I'll give you a head start!'

And off they went, shouting and laughing, running across the field, working off their youthful energy and high spirits.

Like any other kids.

In the Thorn household, the mansion was being put to rest for another winter. The maids shook out voluminous white dust-covers and placed them over the furniture, making the house a mixture of museum and mortuary.

Ann came out of the dining room and hurried up the wide marble stairs that led to the second-floor bedrooms. Supervising this particular part of the Thorns' annual routine always depressed her, so she tried to get through it as quickly as possible.

When she reached the second floor, she approached the maids collecting the dirty linen from the various bedrooms. She singled out one in passing.

'Is Miss Marion dressed yet, Jennie?'

The maid shook her head. 'I don't think she's awake, Mrs Thorn. I knocked earlier, but she didn't answer.'

'Thank you,' Ann said as she brushed past Jennie and headed for Aunt Marion's door. When she got there, she rapped twice, sharply.

There was no answer.

Ann cocked her head to listen but heard nothing. 'Aunt Marion,' she said, 'you don't want to miss your plane!'

Still nothing.

Ann decided to go in. She tried the door and found it open. She entered the room quietly.

She didn't see Aunt Marion right away. There was no one in the bed. The sheets were twisted this way and that, evidence that the occupant had spent a sleepless night.

It was not until Ann had crossed to the other side of the bed on her way to the bathroom that she finally saw Aunt Marion, lying sprawled on the rug near the bed. Her body was contorted in such an unnatural way that it was clear she was dead. Her well-worn Bible lay open and face down, inches away from one outstretched hand.

Ann clamped a hand to her mouth to keep from screaming. She closed her eyes tightly and turned away, as if to try to erase the image from her mind. She wished they hadn't had such a fight the night before. It seemed so silly and pointless now.

When she opened her eyes, she noticed for the first time the open window with its pale lace curtains blowing softly in the early morning breeze.

The area south of Chicago, and west of Cicero, Illinois, becomes one long, flat expanse, like Kansas. There, in an otherwise entirely rural section, was the new plant that Buher wanted Thorn Industries to buy. Its long glass walls seemed to stretch into infinity, a low-lying science-fiction presence in a nineteenth-century landscape.

The Thorn Industries helicopter fluttering down onto the open field seemed like science fiction, too, as did the electric buggy waiting for it – a sort of super golf cart with television and a CB radio system installed inside.

The cart was driven by David Pasarian, chief of Agricultural Research for Thorn Industries. He was the man that Buher had suggested as the best Thorn executive to run the place. A small, swarthy Indian, Pasarian knew from bitter personal experience in his youth what it meant to starve, so he was perhaps the most highly motivated member of the Thorn agricultural team. This team was constantly on the lookout for new methods to feed what, to Pasarian's enormous resentment, was called the Third World. Didn't they understand it was all one, and either everyone would eat or everyone would starve?

Pasarian remembered Bangladesh, where he had seen young children with sticklike arms and protruding bellies roaming the streets in packs like wild dogs, willing and even eager to kill for scraps. The separatism that the term 'Third World' implied infuriated him – as did the attitude of his immediate superior, Paul Buher. As far as Pasarian could figure out, Buher didn't see starving children. He only saw percentage points and profit-and-loss statements. He did not understand that statistics were composed of real people who were hungry and who sometimes did extremely dangerous things if they got hungry enough. All Buher understood was that if people got hungry, as they invariably did, and you controlled the food, which is what Buher wanted, then you stood to gain a handsome, steady income. Pasarian hated Buher's cold attitude, but he consoled himself with the thought that if the starving peoples of the world ended up being *fed*, that was all that really mattered.

Pasarian was even willing to put up with Buher's insistence that he chauffeur them in the oversized, over-equipped golf cart. It was a scene out of any of a dozen old Hollywood movies Pasarian had seen projected against the canvas walls of tents when he was a boy; the big silver bird drops out of the sky, the white man comes to save the natives, explaining to them that the volcano is not erupting because they have been evil.

This particular big silver bird, however, was one of the smaller helicopters owned by Thorn Industries, and the white men it bore to earth were Richard Thorn and Bill Atherton. What they had come to explain to the natives was a carefully reasoned position prepared on behalf of the Common Market – another term Pasarian resented. Ten basically white nations ganging up against the basically nonwhite nations of Asia and Africa might be many things, might even be natural – it was certainly the way of the world. But 'common' didn't seem to be the best public relations word to apply to the enterprise.

Pasarian knew enough about the company and the various differences of opinion within it to recognize that this was Buher's big opportunity to convince Richard Thorn that *his* way of doing things was the best way. Pasarian had a private joke with himself that Buher had majored in Persistence and Persuasion in college. He'd never seen anyone like Buher before; always weaseling around, somehow always in the right place at the right time; knowing when to force an opinion and when not to; never giving up, always willing to wait for the right moment. And if it seemed the right moment might never come, doing whatever had to be done to *make* it occur. That was Buher. A real winner type. And a threat to everyone except Thorn, who was exempt only because he owned the damned company, and because as long as he was alive, the predominant philosophy behind Thorn Industries would be his.

The helicopter landed. Everyone shook hands and then the four men took off across the fields in the super golf cart. Pasarian was at the wheel, with Thorn next to him and the other two in back. Buher started making his pitch to Thorn immediately, making sure to denigrate Atherton's opinion right from the start.

'Bill is simply wrong in this area,' he said, leaning forward and shouting into Richard's ear over the noise of the cart's engine. 'My report points to the indisputable fact that Thorn Industries' main interest, at this point in time, is in energy and electronics. What I'm maintaining is that, because of the bias, we tend to ignore the kind of thing that's going on at this plant, for example. And we ignore it at our own risk. Our profitable future, energy aside,' he said, pausing to catch his breath, 'lies in just one thing . . . *famine!* '

Atherton snorted with disgust. 'That statement is typical of you, Paul,' he said, shaking his head. 'It's heartless and –'

'*True!* ' Buher broke in. 'Not heartless. Realistic.'

Atherton leaned in front of Buher, effectively cutting him off, and spoke directly to Thorn. 'Richard,' he said, with great urgency in his voice, 'by 1980, Middle Eastern oil will cost this country twenty billion dollars a year. Prosperity isn't around the corner to begin with, and dollar-a-gallon gas sure isn't going to help. If our responsibility to this nation and to the world at large is *energy,* then we must continue to spend our time and our money on all the alternative forms of it. What about our commitment to the programs we've already begun, in solar energy, gravitational energy, nuclear energy? Are we supposed to turn our backs on the progress we've made so far in those areas and write them off as a well-intentioned waste of our time?'

'Speaking of time, Bill,' said Buher, looking at his watch, 'while you were lamenting our glorious commitment to, and future in, the energy business, eight people starved to death. One person dies of starvation somewhere in the world every eight point six seconds. Seven every minute. Four hundred and twenty every hour. Ten thousand every day.'

Atherton didn't even bother to disguise his contempt or outrage. 'What is your *point,* Paul?'

'My point, Bill,' said Buher, with exaggerated impatience, as though he were explaining things to a child, 'is that it doesn't make much sense to create new sources of energy if no one's going to be alive to use them.'

Thorn decided it was time to step in. 'Isn't that a little bleak?' he asked.

'The day is coming, Richard,' Buher said with total conviction. 'Sooner than you think.'

'Go on,' said Thorn. He realized that Buher often exaggerated his case, but the fact was that the man's instincts were uncannily sound. And anyway, it was always best to hear all sides, no matter how extreme.

Buher let out an almost comic sigh of relief. 'I thought you'd never ask,' he said.

Atherton sat back in his seat, crossed his arms, and sulked. Pasarian had to smile. Some days it was sincerity, today it was theatrics. Whatever method Buher chose to use, he almost always got his way.

And as the golf cart drove on toward the enormous greenhouse that was its destination, the four occupants were too preoccupied to notice the guard who was waving at them wildly. He was trying to get Richard Thorn's attention, for an extremely urgent phone call had just come in for him.

Once inside the greenhouse, the four men walked down a long passageway in a seemingly endless sea of green. They were totally silent, awestruck at what lay before them. It was an incredible sight; oversized vegetables grew on one large table, while miniature windowbox farms thrived on another. Buher could see that even Atherton was moved, and he was inwardly ecstatic. For the time being, however, he maintained his air of reserve and continued his presentation in a hushed tone that was almost prayerful.

'There was a man once,' he said, 'who asked, "Can you plow the sea?" ' People thought he was mad. But he wasn't, he was just ahead of his time. The answer to his question is "Yes." Not only can we, but we must. And hydroponics is only the beginning of it.' They all moved farther down the passageway, past plots of vegetables that were far more brightly colored than it seemed they had a right to be. Finally they reached a section where there were some technical exhibits, charts, and graphs.

'Here,' said Buher, pointing out an elaborate, perfectly scaled-down model, 'you see the modern farmer as he *will* be. He sits at a control console in this central tower. He receives information about his fields from television and memory computers. His plowing has been done for him by ultrasonic waves beamed down from small, remote-controlled aircraft. His computer machines can pick, grade, and box fruit with computer-controlled mechanical fingers.'

Finally Atherton found his tongue. 'And what will that do for the starving Chinese?'

'*Feed them*!' Buher shouted with terrible intensity. 'The Chinese pride themselves on the fact that they can march all day on a bowl of rice, but what kind of accomplishment is *that*? We have to feed these people!' Now Buher really began to hit his stride. 'And to do that, the oceans must be farmed, new strains of faster-growing rice must be developed, imitation meat must be manufactured. And we – Thorn Industries – *must* take the lead. We will own the land, or rent it. We will own or control a percentage of the crops and the animals. We will manufacture the fertilizers that make food grow, and we will design and build the machinery that will turn barren land and polluted seas into arable, plentiful gardens.'

'And what would *you* be?' Atherton asked contemptuously. 'Czar of this utopia?'

Buher was not in the least offended. Speaking half to himself, as he looked off into the green universe through which they had just passed, he said slowly, 'Do you know . . . there was a very primitive tribe once, high up in the mountains of Mexico, who lived on very good soil, but they simply lacked the technology to till it. An American construction company was there, building roads, and just before they left, they gave a tractor to the natives and showed them how to operate it. And after the natives had learned to plow their fields, do you know what they did with the tractor?'

'They ate it,' said Pasarian, speaking up for the first time that morning.

It was not clear whether Buher missed the sarcasm or chose to ignore it. 'They built a church around it,' he said, answering his own question, 'and they hoisted it up on an altar, and they got down on their knees before it, and they *worshipped* it.'

Atherton suddenly felt cold.

Just then, a white-coated technician ran up to the group. 'Excuse me, Mr Thorn,' he interrupted. 'You're wanted on the telephone. It's urgent.'

Richard thanked the technician and excused himself from the group. The heated discussion continued as he headed off to take the call.

'The oil countries didn't hesitate to put the knife to our jugular vein, did they?' asked Buher. 'What's so different about food?' He held out his hands as if to say, What else can we do? 'If there's a knife at your belly, you keep your hands at your side, right? Control. *Organization.* Why call my policy unethical? It's the only alternative left to us in a world of increasing complexities!'

Atherton was still not convinced. 'If we're going to make tenant farmers out of the hungry peoples of the world,' he said, his patience wearing thin, 'why not go all the way and turn them into slaves?'

'Customers,' said Buher emphatically. 'And the point is, we'd keep their bellies full.'

As much as he disliked Buher's manner, Pasarian's main concern had always been, and would always remain, the feeding of his people. 'I have to agree with Paul,' he said. 'I think we should move in this new direction.'

Just then Richard returned, pale from yet another

crisis. 'Marion died in her sleep last night,' he said. 'Coronary occlusion.'

Atherton was genuinely shocked. 'Oh, Richard!' he said, 'I'm so sorry!'

Thorn nodded his thanks, his mind already considering all the things that would now have to be done. 'I'm afraid I have to leave,' he said, turning to Atherton. 'Can you drive me to the helicopter?'

Atherton nodded. 'Of course.'

'Paul,' Thorn continued, 'please get to a phone right away and notify the board of directors. And see to it that a cable is sent to every overseas executive above the status of plant manager.'

'Will do,' said Buher.

'I'll hold a board meeting in ten days. The funeral is in three. No flowers, contributions to the Heart Fund instead. And I'll take care of the banks and the Street.' Richard shook hands all around, then started to leave with Atherton.

Buher caught him by his coat sleeve. 'Richard?' he asked. 'Could we have breakfast tomorrow morning to finish discussing this project?'

Atherton was appalled, but Thorn took it in stride. 'Of course,' he replied. 'Come by the apartment around eight.' Then he moved away, with Atherton not far behind.

Pasarian shook his head at Buher. He certainly didn't waste any time, did he? An old woman dies. So what, Buher would probably say, the rest of us live on. And Buher would continue to press his ideas on Richard Thorn until the company was operating on a basic philosophy that was essentially *his*.

Buher interrupted Pasarian's train of thought. 'The Thorns have already moved into the city then?' he asked.

Pasarian nodded. 'Today.'

'Winter's here again,' Buher said.

He walked off in search of a phone in order to carry out Thorn's instructions.

Even in her last act, Marion Thorn had proved to be a terrible inconvenience.

At that moment, thirty thousand feet over the Atlantic Ocean, not far from the Straits of Gibraltar, an El-Al jet was speeding west, after having taken off from the airport at Tel-Aviv.

On board, back behind the left wing in the tourist section, sat a very attractive English woman, with auburn hair and flashing eyes. Her name was Joan Hart. And just as Dr Warren had said, she was on her way to America to try to interview the elusive Richard Thorn. But not for the reasons he supposed.

Ever since the sudden disappearance of her friend and lover, Michael Morgan, seven years earlier, Joan Hart had been doing some digging of her own – into the past, into the Bible, and into the facts surrounding the series of odd deaths that seemed to have as their pivot one little boy – Damien Thorn.

And Joan had become convinced of the truth. She felt herself to be a messenger of God. Although Bugenhagen had chosen Michael Morgan as his spiritual successor, that choice had come to naught. But Joan had been at their meeting, too. She had heard everything, and she believed that her being there had not been merely a coincidence. Just as there had been a reason for her presence in the café on that sultry afternoon in Acre seven years before, so now there was a mission in her life – to see to it that this new Anti-Christ did not live past his thirteenth birthday. For on that day he would know who he was, and it would become all the more difficult, if not impossible, to destroy him thereafter.

As all the Cassandras of the world had been treated in their time, so Joan was now. No one believed her.

Everyone who knew her laughed and said it was just another one of her passing fancies. Those who didn't know her thought she was insane.

And Joan hadn't been so sure of her sanity either – until the week before. She had been assigned to write a special story on the dig at Belvoir Castle, something she had long been waiting for. She had been there when they found the bones of two twentieth-century human males, both of whom she was sure she could identify. She also had gotten a good look at Yigael's Wall.

It was then that she had realized she wasn't mad. It was then that she finally understood and believed. And it was then that she determined to fly to the States to confront Richard Thorn with the truth, and to warn all those who were in the most immediate danger that the Son of the Devil lived right in their midst.

It was not an easy task, but it was one she looked forward to with the rapturous sense of mission that is typical of all true believers.

CHAPTER THREE

The dining room of the Thorns' Chicago apartment was elegantly handsome with its dark wood paneling and its soft brown leather, chrome and glass furniture. Thorn usually started his day in the light and airy breakfast room adjacent to the kitchen, but as this was a private business breakfast with Buher, he had decided to hold the meeting in the quieter and more formal dining room.

Halfway through their grapefruit, the two men were still discussing topics other than the one for which the meeting had been scheduled.

'And when do you plan to open the exhibit?' asked Buher, pretending a polite interest in Thorn's archaeological hobby. Before Thorn could answer, an impeccably dressed butler entered carrying a silver tray impressive enough to be worthy of bearing the Hope Diamond at least, instead of the soft-boiled eggs in porcelain cups that it actually held.

'That depends on when the last of the crates arrives from abroad,' Thorn said, 'but we're aiming for Easter.'

Thorn waited until the butler had removed the first-course dishes before turning the conversation to the real matter at hand.

'Paul,' he began, 'your report's brilliant, and how you turned it out in a month I'll never know.'

Buher was too well versed in corporate ways not to recognize a gentle letdown when he heard it. '*But . . .*' he said, saving Thorn the trouble of saying it.

Thorn smiled. '*But* . . . I don't think it's proper to

enter into a project that radical without the full support of all our top people.'

'And Bill Atherton is against it.'

'Yes, and I trust him. You should, too. He might not be a dazzler like some of these young hot-shots, but he knows what he's doing.' Thorn paused to sip his coffee. 'I wish you'd make more of an effort to get along with him,' he went on. 'It would make your progress around here a hell of a lot easier.'

Buher knew that what he was about to say was dangerous, but he decided to risk it. One never got ahead by being cautious. 'Richard,' he said, leaning forward in his chair, 'if Bill Atherton's antagonism toward me is going to continue – if my career here is going to depend on keeping in the good graces of a man who obviously doesn't like me – perhaps it would be best for all concerned if I resigned. Left the company.'

'Nonsense,' Thorn said. Then, with a smile, he added, 'Your time will come.'

Buher nodded, but kept his own smile inside. 'All right,' he said, 'I'll keep my thoughts on ice for the time being.'

Until my time *does* come, he thought.

When they had finished breakfast, Buher followed Thorn out to the limousine, which was waiting to take him to the airport. Thorn had a meeting in Washington, which, despite Aunt Marion's death, could not be put off.

As they shook hands good-bye, Thorn softened the rejection he had just dealt Buher by saying, 'You'll be coming to the boys' birthday party this weekend, won't you? Up at the lake house?'

'Wouldn't miss it for the world,' said Buher, playing the same gentlemanly game as his employer. 'Is the lake frozen yet?'

'You bet,' said Thorn, putting his hand on Buher's shoulder. 'Bring your skates.'

Buher smiled and waved, then turned to walk to the corner to catch a cab. He had to laugh when he thought of Bill Atherton, in a business suit and tie, overcoat and muffler, stumbling about on the frozen surface of the Thorn's private lake. It should be fun.

Just as he had his hand on the limousine door, which Murray was holding open for him, Thorn heard a voice, distinctly feminine and obviously English, calling, 'Mr Thorn? Oh, Mr Thorn!'

He turned and saw an extremely attractive young woman waving to him excitedly as she crossed the street. She was wearing a bright red wool coat, with an equally bright red fluffy fur collar, red gloves, and high-heeled black leather boots; a large black leather bag hung over one shoulder. Her smile was dazzling but somewhat forced.

For a moment, Thorn was completely puzzled. The woman looked familiar and yet he knew he had never met her. Then he remembered where he had seen her before: in one of Warren's slides, standing beside the statue of the Whore of Babylon.

It was Joan Hart, the journalist.

Thorn's pleasure at such a pretty woman eager to see him vanished instantly. This was a reporter who, Warren had said, wanted to interview him. But before he could escape into his limousine, she was at his side.

'Sorry to shout at you like that,' she said, 'but I didn't want to let you get away . . .'

'That's all right,' Thorn said politely, but with a good deal of reserve. He knew why she was there, and he had no intention of giving her what she wanted.

'My name's Joan Hart,' she said. 'I believe Charles Warren told you about me.'

'Yes, he did,' said Thorn. 'I asked him to tell you –'

'He told me,' she interrupted, then changed her tone. 'It's absolutely freezing out here. Couldn't we possibly sit in your car while you tell me why you won't let me interview you?'

Thorn had to smile. 'You would have made a great Avon lady.' And then, with a welcoming gesture toward the capacious back seat of the limousine, he said, 'Get in.'

As soon as they were both settled comfortably in the back of the car, Joan Hart began to grope around in her bag, which looked to Richard as though it could easily have contained all the research for her book about Bugenhagen. She produced an expensive silk handkerchief most woman have been proud to wear as a scarf, and blew her nose.

'I'm an absolute wreck on a cold day,' she said.

'Miss Hart –' Thorn began.

'I know. You never talk to reporters.'

'And I'm on my way to the airport –' he said.

'Two minutes,' she said. 'That's all I ask. Please.'

'I can't miss my plane. If you want to see me another time –'

'I thought planes waited for Richard Thorn,' she said.

'Not this one.'

'Then I'll ride to the airport with you.' She flashed an irresistible smile. 'Where are you going?'

Thorn pressed the button on the intercom that allowed him to speak to Murray through the thick glass partition that separated them. 'Let's go, Murray,' he said. Then, clicking off the intercom, he answered Joan Hart's question: 'Washington.'

Joan Hart smiled again. 'Air Force One waits for no man. What are you doing, advising the President on how to run the country?'

'No,' said Thorn, finding that he enjoyed her sense

66

of humor more than he wanted to. 'Just the Secretary of State. Now, what can I do for *you*?'

Joan Hart reached into her bag again and brought out a small leather-bound notebook and a gold pencil. Her manner changed instantly, as if possession of the notebook invested her with special powers. She was transformed into the hard, smooth professional reporter, digging away at the hidden facts, like Bugenhagen excavating artifacts.

By the time they were halfway to O'Hare, Thorn was tired of the interview game. 'You've asked me seven questions so far, Miss Hart,' he said, 'and every one of them has to do with money.'

She favored him with her most devastating smile. 'Makes the world go round, doesn't it?'

'That, and a few other things,' Thorn said.

Joan could tell he was getting restless and annoyed, but she couldn't tell him what she believed. Not yet. She needed a little more time.

'Uh . . . your father built the museum in –' she glanced at her notes – '1940, I think it was. How much did it cost?'

'About ten million, more or less,' said Thorn.

'Give or take a million,' she laughed. 'When your father first came to Chicago, didn't he work in the stockyards?'

'Right.'

'And didn't he make you and your brother Robert take cold baths and sleep on boards so you'd know what it was like to be poor?'

Thorn burst out laughing. 'Is that what they tell you about us?'

Just then, the limousine stopped short. They had come to the Michigan Avenue drawbridge that crosses over the Chicago River. Its strident warning bells and flashing red lights signaled that the bridge was about to be raised to let a ship pass. Thorn looked out the car window and recognized a Thorn Industries tanker. He was being delayed by one of his own ships.

Joan Hart chose that moment to change the subject. She took the raising of the drawbridge to mean that she had been granted the time she needed to tell Thorn what she had come to tell him.

'Did you ever meet Bugenhagen?' she asked.

'No,' said Thorn, sensing immediately that she had taken a different tack.

'Did you know he was an exorcist as well as an archaeologist?'

'I don't see what that has to do with —'

'His skeleton was found in your dig at Belvoir Castle,' she went on. 'Didn't you know that?'

'*A* skeleton, Miss Hart. It hasn't been officially identified yet as Bugenhagen's.'

Joan Hart spoke with chilling conviction. '*Two* skeletons, Mr Thorn. One was Bugenhagen's, the other belonged to a young archaeologist named Michael Morgan. Michael Morgan was my fiancé, Mr Thorn. I was with him the day he disappeared. With Bugenhagen.'

Just then, the barricade was lifted and Murray started the car. Thorn jabbed the intercom button furiously.

'Murray, stop the car. Miss Hart is getting out.'

Joan Hart spoke in a rush now: 'The week before your brother died, he flew to Israel to see Carl Bugenhagen. A few days after *his* death, Bugenhagen and Michael Morgan were buried alive. Doesn't it make you wonder, Mr Thorn?'

Just what I need, Thorn thought, a conspiracy nut. In a minute, she'll be telling me who killed the Kennedys. In a tight, controlled voice, he said, 'Don't make me throw you out, Miss Hart. We're blocking traffic.'

'You know why the police shot your brother, don't

you, Mr Thorn?' Joan Hart's face took on the look of true madness. Her eyes glinted wildly. 'You know about the daggers, don't you?'

Murray was out of the car, holding the door open for her.

'All I know, Miss Hart,' said Thorn, 'is that you're wasting my time and your own.'

'Please listen to me!' Joan Hart was pleading now. 'I've been working on the story for years! I think I've pieced it together –'

Richard Thorn groaned. Not this all over again. He had thought the details of the bizarre religious aspects surrounding his brother's death had been successfully suppressed. But apparently not.

Murray reached in and took Joan Hart by the arm, a bit more roughly than was necessary. Struggling to stay in the car, she shouted at Thorn, 'You're in grave danger!'

'Get away from me,' Thorn snapped back at her. 'Don't ever come near me again. Do you understand?'

'Turn to Jesus!' she begged.

'Murray, for God's sake!'

'Put your faith in Christ!' she sobbed.

Murray all but lifted her out of the car and slammed the door shut behind him. Even as he set her down on the street, she was shouting: 'Yes! For *God's* sake! Only He can protect you! Look at the paintings on Yigael's Wall, Mr Thorn! Look at the face of Satan and tell me whose face it is!'

'Murray, get me the hell away from this crazy woman!' Thorn shouted.

Murray jumped in the car and started the motor. As the car pulled away, Joan Hart ran after it, banging on the back window and screaming, 'Listen to me! You've got to listen to me!'

But the car was going too fast for her to follow. She stopped running and stood in the middle of the road, tears of fear and frustration streaming down her face, the cold wind whipping her bright red coat around her shivering body.

When Reginald Thorn made up his mind to erect a monument to himself, he decided that a museum would be suitable, and he went to an old friend, who had been an associate of the great Chicago architect, Louis Sullivan, to discuss it.

Thorn explained that he wanted a neoclassical building, something that would not look dated in a few years. He also did not want an older architect to design the building. He wanted someone young, brash, full of himself and full of new ideas. He trusted his friend to come up with the right young man.

His friend did not fail him. He introduced Thorn to an assistant in his office, a former protégé of Frank Lloyd Wright, and the plans for the Thorn Museum got underway immediately.

Now, almost forty years later, The Thorn Museum looked as new and handsome as if it had been designed and built the week before. It stood on the shore of Lake Michigan, just off the most expensive and prestigious stretch of Michigan Avenue, and it suffered not at all from comparison with the Mies van der Rohe buildings that were its neighbors.

As Joan Hart's cab pulled up in front of the museum, posters everywhere proclaimed the current exhibition of Edvard Munch paintings. The posters featured Munch's most famous and horrifying work, 'The Scream.' Joan Hart stood and stared for a long time at the masterpiece before she walked up the ramp leading into the museum. It seemed to her that the painting was not merely apt but was actually another sign that she was on the right track, and she drew encouragement from it.

Inside, dwarfed by the high ceiling, she suddenly felt small and vulnerable once again. But she knew why she had come and what she was looking for. A guide directed her to the gallery on the second floor where Charles Warren was preparing his exhibition of artifacts from the ill-fated Bugenhagen dig at Belvoir.

Warren stood amid a welter of floor plans and photographs; he was showing Ann Thorn how he planned to install the exhibition. Although Ann often interested herself in the affairs of the museum, having selected that as her special province from among her husband's many concerns, Warren had never seen her as consumed with curiosity as she was about the artifacts arriving from Acre.

'We're going to reconstruct the catacomb at the end, there,' he said, pointing to a floor plan. 'That way, as the visitors move from one gallery to the next, they will constantly glimpse it in the distance. Each time it'll be closer, until finally they'll have to go through it just as they leave the exhibiton.'

'That's very imaginative,' Ann said.

Warren smiled his thanks. 'I'm told they found something after I left, something called Yigael's Wall. They'll send it as soon as it's ready.' He pointed to another room on the floor plan. 'I'm keeping this far gallery in reserve, just in case.'

Ann's interest grew more intense at the mention of Yigael's Wall. 'Who exactly was this Yigael?' she asked.

'A rather mysterious character,' said Warren. 'A monk and an exorcist. Supposed to have lived in the thirteenth century. The story goes that Satan appeared to him, and, not unexpectedly, he went out of his mind.'

Warren had expected Ann to laugh at that – it was most people's reaction – but, to his surprise, she did not. So he went on with his explanation: 'He then went into hiding. Apparently he was so obsessed with the face of Satan that all he could do was paint the Anti-Christ, as only he had seen Him, from His birth until His downfall.' Warren shrugged. 'I guess he was determined to leave the world a record of his vision. Yigael himself was never seen again. Only his wall.'

'I can't wait to see it,' said Ann excitedly. She was fascinated by Warren's stories and bits of historical background.

'And now,' Warren said, pointing at the floor plan once again, 'for your favourite piece – the Whore of Babylon! We're putting it right here in the middle of Room Four, so that no one can miss it.'

In the midst of their discussion, Joan Hart suddenly entered the room.

Warren looked up. 'Joan!' he said with both surprise and delight in his voice. 'This is perfect! When did you get in?'

'Last night.' She smiled nervously. She was trying to disguise the urgency she felt.

'Ann,' Warren said, drawing her into the conversation, 'this is Joan Hart, the young lady –'

'– in your slide,' Ann finished. She had a photographic memory when it came to other beautiful women.

Warren nodded. 'Standing beside the Whore of Babylon.'

Ann thought of several quick replies to that remark but decided against using any of them. Instead, she said, 'I'm Ann Thorn. You're the one who wanted to interview my husband.'

'I did interview him,' Joan said.

Warren was furious. All the pleasantries were instantly forgotten. 'I explicitly told you –' he began.

But Joan cut him off. 'You didn't understand how important this was to me,' she said. 'I just couldn't take no for an answer.'

'You must be very persuasive,' Ann said, her tone less than friendly. 'How did you manage to get to him?'

Joan could be bitchy when she wanted to, and Ann was making her want to. 'I threw myself at him!' she said, mustering as much charm as she could. 'Right into his big shiny car.

'Did you?' Ann said. 'I'm sure he enjoyed that.'

'Well, not at first,' said Joan, implying that the interview had ended well. For some reason, she wanted to make Ann jealous. She couldn't decide why, but there was something about Ann she didn't like at all. And she had liked Thorn very much, until he'd become afraid and had her thrown out of his car. 'He doesn't have a very high opinion of reporters, does he?' she went on.

'He thinks they live off other people's misfortunes,' said Ann, not bothering to disguise the fact that it was her opinion as well.

Joan's smile was, if possible, even more dazzling than before. 'Like jackals?' she asked. She was testing Ann, trying to find out how much she knew.

'What a good comparison,' said Ann with a straight face, leaving no hint as to whether she understood the allusion or not.

Warren was distinctly unsettled by this clash, which he only dimly understood, and he tried to set it right. 'Joan writes mainly about archaeology,' he offered. As soon as he'd said it, he realized how lame a comment it was.

Ann gave the remark the level of consideration it deserved. 'Does she?' she said, and smiled her killer smile.

Warren's pocket beeper beeped shrilly, a ludicrous note in the chilly atmosphere. Most of the time he resented the little device; it tied him to Thorn Industries like an umbilical cord he longed to cut. At this particular moment, however, he was grateful for the excuse it gave him to leave. 'Back in a moment,' he said, and left the ladies to settle their differences without him.

'You know,' said Joan Hart casually, 'your husband is

a little unfair to the press. They were very kind to his brother.'

'What do you mean?' Ann asked sharply, beginning to wonder what the woman was after.

'Their reporting of his death was most circumspect,' said Joan Hart blandly. 'After all, the circumstances were a bit unusual.'

'Were they?' asked Ann calmly, trying to remain poised under pressure. 'I never knew Richard's brother.'

Joan looked as though a thunderbolt from heaven had just burst through the ceiling and struck her. 'That's right!' she said, 'I keep forgetting! You're Richard's second wife!'

'Miss Hart –' Ann began.

'Now let me get this straight,' Joan went on. 'Damien is his brother's son, and Mark is his son by his first wife. In fact, you're neither boy's mother!'

'You should be writing for the women's page!' Ann said sarcastically, her control beginning to collapse.

'And Damien,' Joan persisted, 'tell me about him. What kind of boy is he? Is he enjoying the military academy?'

Before Ann could respond, Charles Warren burst into the room. 'Ann!' he shouted. 'Don't say another word to that woman!' He grabbed Joan roughly by the shoulders and led her toward the door. 'You've made a fool of me,' he said, more upset than anyone had ever seen him. 'Richard's furious!'

Joan had nothing more to lose. 'You're in danger!' she said in a hushed, desperate tone. 'All of you!'

'What has gotten into you?' Warren struggled to get her out of the room, away from Ann and any further embarrassment.

'I've seen Yigael's Wall!' she said, as if that explained everything.

It had no effect on Warren, who continued to hustle her out. 'I don't care what you've seen!'

'But you *must* care!' Joan wrenched herself free from Warren's grasp and turned toward Ann. 'Damien –'

'What about Damien?' asked Ann sharply.

'He . . . he . . .' Joan started to speak, then suddenly, inexplicably, changed her mind. 'I don't know!' She ran from the room.

The two watched in stunned silence as Joan ran down the long corridor and disappeared around the far corner. Ann turned slowly back to Warren.

'What the hell was that all about?' she asked.

Warren shook his head sadly. 'I have no idea,' he said. 'Jesus loves everybody, but some very strange people love Him!'

Warren had been serious, but Ann found his remark the funniest thing she had heard in ages. When her laughter subsided, she gave him a big hug, and the two of them went back to work on the exhibit, all but forgetting that Joan Hart had ever set foot in the room.

Although it had appeared to both Warren and Ann that Joan Hart, wild and distracted, had rushed blindly out of the museum, with no idea of where she wanted to go or what she wanted to accomplish, they could not have been more wrong.

She had never in her life been more purposeful. Pursued by demons, and, in her view, pursuing one, she knew exactly what she had to do. The same impetus had brought her across the ocean from Tel-Aviv, and she was not about to stop just because people here in America also thought her insane.

She went straight to the nearest Avis office; their slogan, 'We Try Harder,' appealed to her in her present frame of mind. She rented a car and drove with speed and determination north of Chicago. By early afternoon, she was at the military school where Mark and Damien Thorn were enrolled. She arrived during a practice session of the football team.

Davidson Military Academy placed great importance on physical fitness. Their concern went far beyond the *mens sana in corpore sano* philosophy common to most schools. At Davidson, the supposition, of course, was that the cadets might actually grow up to be soldiers and fight for their country one day. A strong, healthy body was very important to the military way of thinking; it made a better instrument for killing. In any case, there was no room in the trenches for overweight soldiers.

Moreover, if, as was far more likely, these boys grew up to be like their fathers, spending their lives talking on the telephone and going to lunch with other men like themselves, strong, healthy bodies would be far more able to withstand the rigors of alcohol, cholesterol, and starch, not to mention the lack of regular exercise. Either way the approach was practical.

But the goals of Davidson were of no interest to Joan Hart. She was consumed by her own obsession: she was about to look on the face of Damien Thorn and would shortly see how closely it resembled the deranged vision of the mad painted Yigael, beside whose masterpiece her lover's bones had rested for seven years.

If the players on the football field had been a few years older, her sudden appearance might have brought on catcalls and caused minor havoc. She was certainly the most attractive female to have set foot on the grounds of Davidson Military Academy in a long time, and the intensity of her face made her all the more attractive.

But there was no one to notice: the only spectators were a few parents there to cheer on their respective sons. They sat in isolated groups in the bleachers, totally focused on the game; from time to time they stamped their feet against the cold, as their breath came out in small smokelike puffs in the brisk afternoon air.

Neff, of course, was the right age to notice Joan, but

he was watching the play between the two young teams as intently as if he were coaching the Super Bowl. And even had he noticed her, he would have been immune to her flashy red coat and her dry English charm.

Joan Hart noticed a young boy nearby who was obviously a cadet from his uniform, but who was watching the scrimmage instead of playing in it. Her trained eye sized up the situation instantly; the boy was scrawny, he had pimples, and he wore glasses with lenses as thick as plate-glass windows. His attention was riveted on the field. Perhaps he felt an adolescent, semihomosexual attraction to the smooth, lean youths out there. Obviously one of them was his hero.

If Joan Hart had been in a different frame of mind, she would have been willing to bet a fair sum of money on who that hero was. But considering the circumstances, she wanted to know only one thing. She wanted to know if Damien Thorn was on the field, and if so, which one he was. It was virtually impossible for her to distinguish individual features under the heavy protective helmets.

She was just about to ask the scrawny cadet her question when Neff called for a break in the play. Intent on her mission, Joan failed to notice. She tapped the boy on the shoulder, breaking his intense concentration, and asked rather loudly, 'Is Damien Thorn playing?'

Before the boy had a chance to answer, one of the players on the field turned to look at Joan. His eyes seemed to bore into her back. She felt his gaze and whirled around to look. She thought she recognized the eyes, although she had seen them painted as baleful yellow cat's eyes, full of electricity and lacking irises.

With that, the player suddenly took off his helmet, and Joan Hart saw the same sharp-planed face she had seen in the painting at Acre.

'That's Damien Thorn,' the young cadet said, pointing, but Joan Hart already knew.

She backed away in horror. Her lovely face, now twisted and stricken, reflected the expression of a person who believes implicitly in the existence of the Devil and who has just seen Him in human form.

She turned and began to walk slowly away from the playing field in a pathetic attempt to appear casual. But before she had gone very far, terror overcame her, and she found herself breaking into a full run, her legs flying as she covered the seemingly enormous distance that lay between her and the car.

Her back felt hot again, just below the shoulder blades, and strangely, she knew at once the reason. It was there that Damien Thorn's horrid yellow eyes were zeroing in on her.

When she finally reached the sanctuary of her rented car, she heard a voice – Neff's – say sharply: 'Get your ass over here, Thorn.'

And then the hot areas on her back disappeared. She fumbled in her bag for the car keys, found them, missed the key slot twice, finally got it right, heard the motor kick over, and drove, tires screeching, away from Davidson Military Academy. Away from the terrifyingly familiar face of Damien Thorn, whom she had never seen in the flesh before.

She kept driving north. She didn't know why. The logical thing to do was to turn around and go back to Chicago, but she knew there was no help for her there. She had no chance of ever again being allowed into the presence of the Thorns, both of whom thought her a madwoman. Charles Warren had been her best hope. She knew he believed in Jesus as much as she did, although not as intensely. And if he believed in Jesus, she thought, he had to believe in the power of the Devil as well. But she knew Charles Warren would not help her, either. Not now. Not after the scene she had caused in the museum. She wondered where the power of Jesus was now. Why wasn't He helping her to convince other people?

It was one thing to sit in a living room or a prayer meeting and ask, 'Do you believe in the existence of Satan?' and have the other person say, 'Yes, of course. He's described in the Book of Revelation.' It was quite another thing to ask a man like Charles Warren to believe that his employer's adopted son was a devil incarnate. Charles Warren was a practical man as well as a Christian; that meant he would practice his Christianity as long as it didn't threaten the security of his job.

Who, then, could she turn to? What aid could she enlist against this most powerful, cunning, and chamelion-like of foes?

Joan Hart continued to drive, operating on a sort of automatic pilot, as she thought about the problem. She wanted to get as far away from Davidson as possible.

In a little while, she had no idea where she was.

She looked up to get her bearings and realized that she had driven far inland. She was in farm country, country as flat as the tiny wafers she had long been accustomed to receiving at Communion on Sunday mornings. She wished she had one now.

She could see the horizon stretching endlessly on all sides of her. Three hundred and sixty degrees of cold, dry flatness. The highway she was on was the only road in sight, and it cut through the flatland with the straight and deadly precision of one of Bugenhagen's knives, which she also dearly wished she had.

The wind came up, moaning, and whipped the trees into frantic motion. Joan, suddenly frightened, decided she had better think about getting back to Chicago, or else finding some kind of lodging for the night.

79

And that was when the car's engine faltered, cut out completely, and died.

The wind died just as quickly.

The car drifted a little bit farther on momentum, then gradually coasted to a halt in the middle of the road.

There was absolute silence. Joan could neither hear nor see any other living thing – no people, no animals, no houses, not even another car in the distance.

She pumped the gas pedal twice in rapid succession and turned the ignition again.

Nothing, not even the sound of a dying battery struggling for life.

She turned the key again several times in rapid succession, but there was not even enough action to flood the motor. She looked at the gas gauge.

Half full.

The trouble obviously lay elsewhere.

She thought about Carl Bugenhagen and Michael Morgan, and how they had died, and she felt a chill that had absolutely nothing to do with the cold.

She suddenly realized what the trouble might be.

Resigned to the fact that it would probably do no good, she stopped trying to start the car. But she was resigned to nothing else. She was extremely agitated; her pulse was racing, her blood pounding in her veins, as she turned over the various possibilities in her mind. She knew she was in grave danger, and she was determined to find a way out of it.

She looked all around, hoping for a sign of life: a car coming, some smoke rising from a distant chimney, even a single cow grazing on the horizon. Anything.

But there was nothing.

She looked in both rear-view mirrors and found the landscape equally bleak and unpromising. The silence was terrifying. Nervously, she switched on the car radio, frustratedly punching one station after another on the dashboard buttons, switching them almost before she had a chance to hear what was on.

She didn't even stop to think that if the battery was as dead as it appeared to be, the radio shouldn't have worked at all.

Just before one station flashed by, she heard a snatch of 'Over The Rainbow' and it made her think of all the times the song had lifted her spirits – had made her feel hopeful and happy. Now it filled her with deep fear, making her feel all the more alone and abandoned.

The next station brought her a fire-and-brimstone politician, rabid, shouting, determined to frighten his listeners into fear of his rivals and into mailing a large check to his own worthy cause. Suddenly his ravings sounded like a foreign language to Joan, like one of the hundreds of voices that were heard at the Tower of Babel, preaching confusion and nonsense.

She felt as if she was going insane.

She switched off the radio and sat there, anxiously drumming her gloved fingers on the steering wheel. She began murmuring under her breath, hardly aware of what she was saying, or even that she was actually praying: 'Our Father who art in heaven,' she whispered, 'hallowed by Thy name, Thy Kingdom come, Thy will be done . . .' Her voice drifted off.

She looked up and down the road again. Still no sign of life.

It was then that she noticed the billboard, although she could have sworn it had not been there a moment before. Old and weatherbeaten, it looked as though it had been standing since the days of Burma Shave roadside poetry. 'Nancy's Place,' it said. 'Good Food at Honest Prices.' And then the most important information of all: '3 Miles.'

Had she been more familiar with the area, she would have known that the section was so totally barren it was more than likely that Nancy's Place no longer existed.

But she chose to believe that within a short walking distance was a restaurant where other human beings were eating and talking and laughing.

She desperately wanted to be one of them. She was sure that she would find help at Nancy's Place. But she would have to walk to get there.

She opened the door and got out of the car. It was much colder than it had been earlier. She turned to reach into the back seat of the car for her coat.

It was then she heard the abrupt fluttering sound, followed by a strange scratching on the roof of her car.

She jumped back. There, not two inches from her face, loomed a huge black raven, staring at her with piercing, malevolent eyes.

She screamed and stumbled backward, struggling to keep her balance. The raven followed her with its eyes, much the same way that Damien had, back at the school. She waved her coat at the raven, but the bird remained where it was, large and unmoving.

She kicked the car door shut and backed away, pulling on her coat against the cold, never once taking her eyes off the raven. There was something deeply horrifying about the bird, and Joan was sure she knew what it was.

The bird had been sent by the Devil.

The raven stayed where it was, motionless, implacable, seemingly secure in the knowledge that it could reach her with one single flap of its wings.

Keeping her eye on the raven, she continued walking backward down the road toward Nancy's Place until she had put a good forty yards between herself and the monstrous bird. Then bowing her head toward the ground and clasping her gloved hands together tightly, she murmured another piece of scripture to herself, almost as an incantation. The passage, from Luke, gave the words of Jesus Himself: 'Behold, I give you power to tread on serpents and scorpions, over all the power

82

of the enemy and nothing shall by any means hurt you!'

Then she whispered, 'Praise the Lord,' and looked up. The raven was *gone*.

Joan Hart let out a shout of joy and relief. What she believed was true, after all! Jesus *did* have the power to dispel evil! She had prayed to Him in His own words, and He had given her the power to tread on scorpions. The large ugly bird, sent by Satan, had been banished by the power of His word. She praised His name.

And at that moment the raven landed on her from behind with a horrendous screech, driving its terrible talons deep into her scalp.

Joan Hart let out a shriek far more piercing than the bird's had been. She beat at the creature, flailed at it with her arms, trying to drive it from her head, but it attacked her arms with its beak and dug in with its claws, embedding them so deeply in her flesh that they could not be dislodged!

Eyes wild and intent with purpose, the raven leaned down over Joan's lovely tear-stained face; it opened its jagged yellow beak wide and pecked at her face again and again, tearing away small pieces of skin with each blow, until its beak was red and dripping with her blood.

Screaming in agony, Joan raised her face to the sky, a sky she could no longer see, imploring someone, *anyone,* to deliver her from this pain. Where her eyes once had been were now two bloody sockets, split open and torn apart, rivulets of blood streaming down her cheeks in a travesty of tears.

Then the raven spread its wings and flew off, soaring high into the sky like an avenging demon from hell, pieces of hair and skin still stuck to its claws.

Reeling in agony, Joan stumbled off the road and slipped down a muddy bank into a ditch. At first she lay there sobbing and twisting about suddenly she lost all energy and lay very still.

Minutes passed.

And then there was a sound, the sound of a diesel engine. In the distance, an eighteen-wheel Peterbilt was coming down the road. Coming fast.

She lifted her head. Was it possible? She scrambled to her feet and tried to find her way back to the road. She slipped in the mud and slid back into the ditch. Her knees were scratched from her fall, and her hands were all covered with blood. She finally made it back onto the roadway. The truck was coming closer. She walked onto the road and started to shout and wave for help.

There is a phenomenon in auditory perception so that if a sound is coming directly *at* you, it is virtually impossible to tell whether it is in front of you or behind. And Joan Hart had no eyes. When the Peterbilt veered around the corner, going much faster than it ought to on such a narrow country road, the driver saw a wild, bedraggled woman standing in the middle of the road and waving for help – *facing the opposite direction.*

The driver had no time. There was nothing he could do.

The eighteen-wheeler barreled right into Joan Hart, tossing her twenty feet into the air like a gaffed fish. She was dead before she hit the ground.

The Peterbilt screeched to a halt a hundred yards down the road.

The silence that followed would have been complete but for the low idling of the truck's engines and the single loud shriek of the raven as it circled higher and higher above, until it seemed to melt away into the distance, into the darkening autumnal sky.

CHAPTER FOUR

Few places in the United States are more beautiful than
the lake region of Wisconsin, and of all the lakes there
many people think that the most beautiful is Lake
Geneva. It is perfectly situated: close enough to
Chicago to be a winter sports center for the wealthy
inhabitants of that city, and yet not so close so as to
suffer from overcrowding on a holiday weekend.

'Lakeside,' the Thorns' winter vacation home on Lake
Geneva, was a big, rambling, natural-wood place styled
like a hunting lodge but with all the modern con-
veniences great wealth makes possible, including such
futuristic embellishments as a helicopter pad and a
closed-circuit television system. Like many wealthy men
with young children, Richard Thorn was forced to
worry about kidnappers, although the TV equipment
had not been installed until the Patty Hearst abduction.

Lakeside also had one of the most sophisticated
telephone systems to be found anywhere in the United
States on nongovernment property. Although he could,
of course, refuse any call he did not wish to take, except
those from the President or the Secretary of State, it
was necessary that Thorn, like most powerful men, be
always available.

The Thorns and some of their friends and business
acquaintances – the groups were, in most instances,
interchangeable, since, with the diversification of Thorn
Industries, there was almost no one with whom Thorn
could not do business – had gathered at the lodge on
Lake Geneva on this particular weekend for the Thorn

boys' thirteenth birthday. The Thorns enjoyed giving parties, especially when they celebrated family birthdays and major holidays.

Although Damien's birthday was actually in June – June sixth, to be exact – ever since he had come to live with his cousin in America, his birthday had been celebrated on the same day as Mark's. Most people assumed this was merely for convenience's sake. Only Richard remembered that his late brother, Robert, in his final madness had attached some strange, arcane significance to that date, and had tried to kill Damien because of it.

The night before the party, Mark and Damien sat playing backgammon in the living room. As usual, Damien was ahead, although Mark seemed to be winning this particular game.

For some reason, Mark was never bothered by losing to Damien. While he *hated* losing to other boys his own age, and he hated it when anyone else beat Damien, where he and Damien were concerned, losing really didn't matter. Perhaps it had to do with Mark's constant, albeit unconscious, awareness of Damien's tragedy-ridden past. Mark had always been unusually sensitive, even as a small child, and now he looked after Damien, in his own fashion, and seemed eager to cheer his cousin on to bigger and better things – sometimes at his own expense.

The two boys sat in front of the large open fire in the enormous brick hearth and rolled the dice. The only sounds were the roar of the fire and the clack of the playing pieces as they were moved around the board. High up on the wall above the boys hung the head of a sixteen-point buck which Richard had shot the year he built the lodge, back when his first wife, Mary, was still alive. His greatest pleasure then had been to come to the lodge and walk in the woods with her. However,

the head of the great deer brought Richard pain whenever he looked at it now; Mary, who could not bear the
death of any living thing, had been horrified the night
he returned from the woods with the buck's dead body
strapped across the hood of his Land Rover. His killing
of the animal, and his stated intention of having its
head stuffed and mounted over the fireplace, had led to
their only serious fight. Mary's mortification led her
to break their unspoken rule about quarrels: that the
argument be limited to whatever had caused it. That
time, though, she had brought up years' worth of petty
and imagined slights. And for a week, Thorn had almost
been afraid she might leave him. Even so, his pride
would not allow him to back down, and he had had
the deer's head stuffed and mounted over the fireplace,
just as he said he would.

When Ann had seen the deer's head for the first time
and asked about it, Thorn had simply told her it was
the head of a buck he had shot and killed in the woods.
The quarrel was one of the few incidents of his first
marriage he had never wanted to discuss with her. Moreover, he knew that he never would. Occasionally, he
wondered why, since Ann, whose love of blood sports
was one of the few masculine things about her, would
almost certainly have sided with him.

The boys were so intent on their game that they didn't
notice when Ann came into the living room. She stood
in silence and watched the two for a while. They really
are such a wonderful pair, she thought. Finally she
broke in on them. 'Hey, you two, it's late. Big day
tomorrow.'

Mark, who was winning for the first time that evening, looked up at her and said, 'We're almost finished
with the game, Mom. Just a few more minutes? Please?'
He looked over at Damien for support.

With a sly grin, Damien, said, 'Come on, Mark. If
Mom says it's bedtime, it's bedtime.'

87

Ann chuckled, knowing exactly what was going on.

Now it was Mark's turn to smile. 'I have an idea,' he said, with a twinkle in his eye. 'Why don't we leave the board standing overnight?'

Everyone laughed as they got up to leave.

After all the good nights and kisses had been exchanged, Ann turned off the light behind them and went to join the other grown-ups. The two boys started up the dark wooden stairs to their rooms.

'Damien,' Mark said, 'I've been meaning to ask you something.'

'Is it *important*?' asked Damien wearily, in perfect imitation of a tired and grouchy businessman.

Mark laughed. 'Of course not,' he said. 'Is it ever?'

'Then go ahead,' said Damien grandly.

'What's with you and Neff?'

Whatever question Damien had expected, that certainly wasn't it. He looked closely at Mark, then said guardedly, 'What do you mean?'

'Well,' Mark replied, stopping at the top of the stairs, 'he seems to be watching you all the time. It's kind of weird.'

'Yeah, it is,' said Damien. He walked down the dark hallway to his room and opened the door. He stopped and turned to Mark, who was still watching him. 'Neff is a sergeant,' he said, 'and all sergeants are weird. Don't you know *anything*?' And then, with a dramatic bow and a smile to show he was only having fun, he stage-whispered, 'Good night,' and disappeared into his bedroom.

By late afternoon the next day, all the guests had arrived. Buher was there, the Pasarian and Atherton, and Dr Warren. Some of the boys from the Academy had even managed to find a way to get up to the lake.

In families like the Thorns – and there are not that many of them in America anymore, perhaps only the

Kennedys and the Rockefellers – the celebration of a birthday, especially a birthday as laden with significance as the thirteenth birthday af a male child, is not so much a social occasion as a tribal rite. A boy is entering into adulthood, about to become a man who, through the exercise of family power, will undoubtedly affect the lives of countless others – perhaps even the destiny of nations. And so the gaiety and lightness with which the Thorns conducted the ceremony was only a social mask, hiding a very real, underlying solemnity.

Mark and Damien, their hands over their faces, stood in the center of the beamed, high-ceilinged dining room, surrounded by family and friends. The lights were dimmed. The air was filled with aromas, mixed, pungent, and subtle, from the splendid buffet that had been laid out on the long refectory table at one side of the room. It was a narrow sixteenth-century table that once belonged to an order of Flemish monks. On a visit to San Simeon, Richard Thorn had noticed the table in one of the dining rooms and had casually remarked to a close friend in the Hearst family how much he liked it. A few weeks later, the table had arrived in Chicago with a note: 'Give me lunch on this thing sometime.' Thorn had been stunned by his friend's generosity but immediately took advantage of the gift and had it shipped up to Lakeside. Now it supported the still considerable weight of the leftovers: smoked turkey, country ham, rare roast beef, salads, corn on the cob, and just about everything else necessary to give two sturdy young boys the strength to become adults.

Only the dessert was missing, and that was on its way.

'Can we look now?' asked Mark, from behind his hands.

'Not yet,' said Ann affectionately.

From the next room came the sound of male voices singing 'Happy Birthday to you, Happy Birthday to you . . .'

'Now?' asked Mark.

'Happy Birthday, Mark and Damien . . .' the male voices sang out.

'Now!' said Ann excitedly, and both boys dropped their hands simultaneously.

'Happy Birthday to you!' The song ended.

What they saw, coming through the double doors from the kitchen, and borne by their father, Atherton, and Pasarian, was a cake that seemed large enough to feed the entire enrollment of Davidson. It looked three stories high, and the top of the cake did not look like the top of a cake at all. It looked like Lake Geneva. In fact, it looked like the area of Lake Geneva that could be seen right through the dining room windows. And skating on the surface of this spun-sugar lake, lit by the thirteen candles that ringed the edge of the cake like night lights around the skating rinks of long ago, was a perfect little three-dimensional Currier and Ives print: turn-of-the-century skaters in long coats and wool mufflers, the women in bonnets, the men in formal high hats, all frozen in mid-step. A man who designed Christmas windows for some of the most exclusive shops in Chicago had been persuaded to apply his artistry to a new medium, and he had created what was certainly the most enchanting, and possibly the most expensive, birthday cake ever seen by anyone, anytime, anywhere. Charles Dickens could have written a chapter about it.

Mark clapped his hands in delight, and Damien broke into smiles. The others responded by giving a round of applause, both to the boys and to the cake, which certainly deserved such attention.

'It's fantastic!' Mark exclaimed, and he was right.

'Happy birthday, darlings,' said Ann, putting her arms around both boys and hugging and kissing them.

Mark, unable to contain himself any longer, finally broke free from Ann's embrace and rushed across the

90

room toward the cake, which the men had just set down on the refectory table. Damien was not far behind.

Just then, Buher came into the room, late for the ceremony. He had had a bad migraine earlier and had gone into another room to lie down for a while. He looked a bit rumpled in his 'casual' clothes, which had actually taken him a good part of the day to assemble. Ann was the first to notice him. She smiled sympathetically. 'Feeling any better, Paul?' she asked.

'Much, thank you,' said Buher. The expression of pain on his face indicated he might not be telling the absolute truth.

'Migraines can be hell,' said Ann. 'I had a friend once who suffered with them. She said she felt as if there were little men in her head with very sharp knives, sawing away through her nerves.'

Buher smiled a smile that would have won him a medal for understated bravery in the good old days when the British still had soldiers in India and no one had to worry about how to feed the starving natives. 'The last few days have been something of a strain,' he acknowledged. He looked across at Atherton who was standing next to the boys and their cake, beaming like the proud uncle he practically was. Mark was happily examining the little figures on the cake, while Damien stuck his finger into the icing and scooped out a large dab of it. Richard stood beside them, a proud and loving father. It was a moving tableau, one in which Buher would have liked very much to play a part.

Mark, naturally ebullient, wanted as many people as possible to share the wonderful sight; he looked up from the cake and called out, 'Mom! Mr Buher! Come and look!'

Ann smiled and went across the room to Mark, while Buher sauntered over in the direction of Damien, who was standing off to one side.

Damien noticed Buher's approach; he smiled and

nodded politely, but he hoped Buher was on his way somewhere else. He didn't feel like talking to grown-ups when there was birthday cake to devour.

'How are they treating you at the Academy, Damien?' Buher asked.

Damien shrugged. 'Okay, Mr Buher.' He tried to indicate by his tone that this was not a topic of particular interest to him, hoping to end the conversation then and there.

'And Sergeant Neff,' Buher asked. 'How is he?'

That got Damien's attention. 'You know him?' he asked, surprise written all over his face.

Buher laughed at Damien's look of shock, and put his hand on the boy's shoulder. 'I asked about him,' said Buher with a smile. 'Just watching over you, Damien.'

Damien didn't quite know what to make of that remark. He half-blushed and turned his attention back to the cake.

But Buher was not so easily dismissed. 'Tell me, Damien,' he said, 'do you know what I do for Thorn Industries?'

Damien looked back at him and shook his head. 'Not really, sir.' He hoped his eyes had glazed over just enough to indicate that he was bored, but not enough so that he seemed totally rude.

'You should,' Buher insisted. 'You should know all about the Thorn holdings. After all, they'll be yours one day.'

'And Mark's,' Damien corrected him.

'I meant "yours" in the plural sense,' said Buher, covering his tracks. This boy is no fool, he thought. Already well trained in diplomacy and tact. He decided to change his approach. 'Why don't you come to the main plant sometime soon?' he said. 'Take a look around.'

The suggestion appealed to Damien. 'Could I bring some friends?' he asked. Immediately he saw a way to

92

get himself and his ever-growing circle of buddies out of class for a day, under the guise of a field trip.

'By all means,' said Buher, as expansive as a ward politician who has just locked up the whole South Side and doesn't much mind if he has to promise box lunches to secure it.

Just then, Richard Thorn tapped the side of a crystal goblet with a silver spoon; the tiny sound brought instant silence to the room as effectively as if he had fired off a gun. Even when he was casually dressed in a wool plaid shirt and a pair of jeans, as he was today, Thorn had an air that commanded attention.

Suddenly, there was champagne for everyone, brought in so unobtrusively that it seemed to have appeared miraculously. As the group assembled at the table, Richard raised his glass in a toast: 'It's at moments like this,' he said, 'that I feel like making a speech, toasting our luck, being thankful for everything we have. Because we do have a great deal. The Thorns are a privileged family and it is essential that we use our privileged position wisely and well. We must never forget that it wasn't always like this, and it won't continue to be like this unless we persist in working hard and in giving hard, to deserve what has been left to us. And that's all I have to say. Mark, you'll be glad to hear I'm not going to make a speech.'

'You just did, Dad,' said Mark, and everyone laughed.

Richard waved his hand to stop the laughter. 'I do have one more thing to say, though.' The gathering groaned in unison. 'Help!' he said, 'I feel like Nelson at the '64 convention.'

By this time, people were roaring with laughter. Tears of mirth rolled down Atherton's face, and Charles Warren was grinning like a Cheshire cat. Looking around, Ann was filled with happy pride; it was turning out to be a wonderful evening.

Undaunted, Richard went on. 'I *am* going to get this

out, no matter how hard you try to stop me.' He paused for effect and to catch his breath. Then, with a grand sweeping motion, he shouted, 'Everybody to the window!'

And everyone did as he commanded, although they were somewhat puzzled. The guests were far behind Mark, however, who, primed for surprises and hoping for another one, had gotten there first.

'Kill the lights, please,' Richard said dramatically when everyone had assembled before the huge picture windows.

The room was plunged in darkness almost before his sentence was completed.

Outside, in the dark night sky, there suddenly appeared, as if by magic – for money can certainly do magical things – one of the most spectacular displays of fireworks that any of them had ever seen. Greens and blues and yellows and reds, brighter than a rainbow, scattered the sky with continual showers of color, lighting up the night into a neon day. There were rockets and streamers and sparklers, all crackling and spitting until they achieved their full height some hundred and fifty feet above the lake, where suddenly they seemed to meld together into bold and sizzling multicolored letters, spelling out:

HAPPY BIRTHDAY, MARK AND DAMIEN!

At first, no one applauded. They were too stunned. They just gasped. And then the clapping and the cheering began, and there were hugs and kisses all around.

'I can't believe it, Dad!' Mark cried, and he ran over to give his father a hug.

Damien just smiled. Although he was just as thrilled as Mark, he couldn't express it as Mark was able to. His emotions were much more internal, much more controlled.

The only person not totally absorbed in the incredible pyrotechnic display was Buher, who once again took the opportunity to single Damien out. He stood directly behind the boy and a little off to one side, so that he could whisper in Damien's ear and not be heard by anyone else.

'A boy's thirteenth birthday,' he said, 'is considered by many as the start of puberty. Of manhood. Jews, for example, have what they call their bar mitzvah. In Hebrew, that means "Son of the Commandment" or "Man of Duty." '

Damien had no idea what he was talking about, but again, he chose to be polite. 'Does it really?' he asked, his gaze still focused on the fireworks.

'You, too, will be initiated,' said Buher.

Damien looked at him. Their eyes locked.

Buher spoke even more softly, almost hypnotically. 'Forgive me if I quote the Bible,' he said, 'but in the First Book of the Corinthians it says, "When I was a child, I spake as a child, I thought as a child; but when I became a man, I put away childish things." The time is coming when you will put away "childish things," when you will face up . . . to who you are.'

'Who I am?'

Buher nodded. 'A great moment, Damien. You must already be feeling it.'

Damien was disturbed but fascinated. At first he had thought Buher was just trying to win him over in order to ingratiate himself with his father. But now Buher, of all people, had just articulated all the turmoil Damien had been feeling over the last few months; it was almost as if Buher could see into his soul. 'I think so,' said Damien slowly. 'I feel . . . I'm not sure, but I feel something's happening to me . . . *going* to happen.' He looked into Buher's eyes to see if that had registered.

Buher smiled. 'Suspicions of destiny, eh? We all have them. Your father, Bill Atherton . . . even myself.' He paused, and then said rather dramatically, 'I am an orphan too, did you know that?'

Damien shook his head.

'So I can share some of what you're going through. You probably first started having these feelings last June, didn't you?' Buher went on, 'When your *real* birthday was . . .'

Damien was astounded, but before he could say anything, Atherton called over to them. 'Hey, you two! Come on and join the fun!'

They looked over and saw that the cake-cutting ceremony had begun.

'C'mon, Damien!' said Mark impatiently. He was all ready to blow out the candles.

'And don't forget to make a wish!' Ann reminded them.

Damien ran to join Mark, relieved, in a way, to break away from Buher. He was burdening him with too much, too soon. Both boys took a deep, deep breath and together managed to blow out all thirteen candles that were spread around the vast circumference of the cake. Everyone cheered as they did so.

'Okay, guys,' said Ann. 'Cut the cake. We're all ravenous!'

'Before we do,' Damien said, 'I have a little something for Mark here.' He started to reach into his pocket.

'Gee,' said Mark slyly, 'I forgot to get you something.' But he was unable to keep a straight face, and reached into his pocket, too.

The boys' presents looked identical in size and shape, even down to the wrapping paper. Mark started to laugh. 'If you got me . . .' be began.

'. . . the same thing I got you . . .' Damien continued.

They both looked at Ann and said, '*Mom*!'

Obviously, 'Mom' had bought both presents. She smiled and looked on happily as both boys eagerly tore open their packages, revealing identical Swiss Army knives, shiny and beautiful and intricate, complete with all the attachments. Everyone cheered again.

'I really wanted one!' said Mark.

'Me, too!' said Damien, as Mark gave him an affectionate shove.

The boys decided to use their birthday knives to cut the cake, but before they did, Damien used his knife to remove one of the male skaters from the winter scene on top. And then both he and Mark plunged their knives deep into the cake, as everyone cheered them on.

The next morning, bright sunlight bounced off the ice on Lake Geneva, bathing the scene in a brilliant glow that refracted into all the shimmering colors of the rainbow. Nature, left to her own devices, had come up with a daytime light show more wondrous than the one Richard Thorn had paid for the night before.

Branching off from the lake, and winding into the surrounding woods, was a river, which was wide at the mouth, then narrowed substantially the deeper it penetrated into the forest. The river was frozen too, and it was here that the hockey games were played. The banks alongside made natural boundaries, keeping the action of the game within a fairly well-defined area.

By afternoon a hockey game was underway, the two teams made up primarily of executives from Thorn Industries. But there were two small ringers on the teams: Mark on one side, Damien on the other, the other boys from the Academy cheering them on.

On the surface the outdoor winter game was all good clean fun; only an executive with antennae as well attuned as Buher's, sensitive to the infinite complexities which affect the emotional temperature of every passing moment, was aware of what was really at stake.

Buher could have pointed out, for instance, that corporate decisions were not made in board rooms; they were only ratified there. They were made at cocktail parties and on squash courts, and, nowadays, most especially on tennis courts. A good backhand was worth three years at Harvard Business School. If you could play well, you got to play with the right people. If you were charming enough, ingratiating enough, and bland enough, your tennis partners would come to consider you their friend, and would therefore prefer to do business with you than with some rank outsider. Careers were made like that. Any Hollywood writer could explain about playing tennis with Jack and Warren and Bob; any ambitious Washington bureaucrat from the Kennedy days could tell about playing squash with Bob MacNamara.

At Thorn Industries, the most popular game was one of the roughest. Quarterbacking, the family skill, might have lent itself to touch football in the autumn air, but the Kennedys had co-opted that game. Basketball was essentially an indoor sport, and when you've spent a week at a desk, the last thing you feel like doing is playing indoors. And Richard, especially after that terrible argument with his late wife, was not about to set up a Hemingwayesque test of manhood by asking some young, upwardly mobile exec to do deer hunting with him. That could have degenerated into a *mano-à-mano* contest, the youngster deferring to his boss, which Richard, with his deeply ingrained sense of taste, would have considered gauche.

No, the Thorn game had to be ice hockey.

The fact that Lake Geneva was so close to the Canadian border undoubtedly had something to do with it. And the hard slam of bodies on the ice substituted nicely for the crunch on the line of a football field. Moreover, the skill of broken-field running pales in comparison to the triple shunts of the finest hockey players.

For all of these reasons, and more, ice hockey became known as the game to play if one wanted to rise in

Thorn Industries. Richard Thorn, who considered himself, and was, in fact, an eminently fair man, would have been shocked had he known that expertise in the game was thought to be of paramount importance by the people in the lower echelons of the company. He would have been appalled had he known that status-wise young executives occasionally spent their Saturday afternoons driving over to Fond du Lac to take lessons from an aging Canadian ex-pro. As far as Richard Thorn was concerned, he was just having a good time.

And today, he was having a particularly good time, as was everyone else. The executives were out in full force; even those who were too old to play were there, braving the cold in a wide and wild variety of outdoor gear.

The wives were present too, decked out in colorful wool caps, boots, and mufflers, their hands encased in mittens, each trying to look as much as possible like the unattainable fantasy girl all young boys have seen and dreamed about at some time in their lives, whether spinning up on the ice, at Rockefeller Center or the local mill-pond.

Damien and Mark were the two captains. They 'shot fingers' to see who got first pick. Damien won, and jumped at the chance to have his foster father on his team. Richard did a funny little skip in place, showing his pleasure at having been the first to be chosen, and then skated over to where Damien was standing.

Mark picked Atherton. He was really not that good at the game, and not in shape for it, but he made up for these deficiencies by his enthusiasm. He smiled in modest appreciation and skated over to join Mark.

Damien picked Buher next. He wasn't sure why he made that choice. Maybe it was some kind of reciprocal gesture, a response to Buher's odd but moving speech of the night before. Or maybe he had a sense that Buher was someone to play *with,* instead of *against.* In any case, Buher seemed extremely pleased to have been chosen by Damien. He sped over toward Damien and Richard and skidded to a sharp stop beside them, spraying chips of ice all over them in the process. He was togged out in the same style of ostentatiously correct casual clothing that had marked him the night before.

Mark's next choice was Pasarian. He liked Pasarian, who was proving himself to be game by simply going out on the ice to begin with. Given his background and training, he was about as much use to a team as a brood mare in a horse race, but his spirit made up for it. He showed signs of being the little Yogi Berra of Lake Geneva ice hockey, doing not much more than cheering, as far as anyone could see, but bringing in a winning team nonetheless.

The rest of the teams were picked, the sides of the playing area chosen, and the game was on.

Buher was an expert player, ruthless and assured. He had obviously practised a great deal. Richard held back, avoiding any star plays because he did not want to be the center of attention. He watched Buher though, and realized – for the first time – that the man had absolutely no sense of 'play.' What was startling to Thorn was that he had never noticed this quality in Buher before. Usually his instincts about people were razor-sharp.

But Thorn didn't dwell on it. He was far too busy watching Damien.

Even in this equivalent of a sandlot game, Damien's skill was astonishing, particularly for a young boy. Flashing about, challenging, delighting in the battle, his skates gleaming in the sun, Damien looked like a *premier danseur* of the ice, a Nureyev on skates. He was magnificent to watch; he controlled the puck most of the time, wielding his stick with style and power, and, to all intents and purposes, he determined the course of play. When Damien smashed through an opening to make the first goal. Richard Thorn smiled with a pride that could have been no more genuine had Damien been his natural son. The shouts and applause from the wives and older executives standing on the shore had nothing at all to do with *who* Damien was; they were seeing virtuosity on display and were responding to the thrill and the beauty of it.

Charles Warren had opted not to play in the game. Instead, he fumbled and stumbled around on his own at the edge of the river, until he got too sore and too tired to keep it up anymore. He shook off the last bit of snow from his latest fall and clumsily skated over to where Ann Thorn stood cooking at a large portable grill.

The silent and all but invisible servants of the night before were excused from duty on the lake today. It was as close to true informality as the Thorns ever got. Ann was cooking vast quantities of hot dogs, hamburgers, and strip steaks over a charcoal fire with the speed and expertise of a great short-order cook. Whatever she had been before she met Richard, she had not been a dilettante at cooking for a crowd; she knew what she was doing here.

Seeing Warren approach, she called out to him: 'What'll it be?'

'Hot dog,' Warren said, puffing.

Ann speared one expertly and poked it into a bun.

'That's all?'

'That's all to *start*,' said Warren. 'I'm famished. I might have to eat this entire spread.'

He gobbled up half the hot dog in one gulp, then paused long enough to load relish, catsup, and onions on what was left.

'I read about your reporter friend in the papers,' said Ann. 'I know it's useless to say I'm sorry, but I am.'

Warren nodded his appreciation. 'I couldn't believe it when I heard the news,' he said. 'I can't imagine how it happened . . .' But Ann had already turned away to watch the game again.

Warren swallowed the rest of the hot dog, then surreptitiously reached for another.

Neither of them noticed the enormous black raven that settled in the branches of a tall, dark tree twenty feet away, regarding them with cold and piercing eyes.

Out on the ice, Richard shot a clear pass to Damien, who stopped it neatly with his stick before sweeping it away and speeding on down the ice toward the goal. Atherton, playing defense, stumbled forward to intercept him, clumsily weighted down with the bulk of his heavy, makeshift cold-weather gear.

Damien charged on ahead, controlling the puck with confidence, enjoying the speed and the finesse with which he was moving. Not for one second did he doubt that he'd be able to dodge the older man. He headed straight for Atherton, traveling very fast, making it look as if he was going to run right through him. Atherton slipped and slid and struggled to hold his position on the ice. He cringed and closed his eyes in exaggerated anticipation of a major collision.

At the very last possible second. Damien executed a perfect pirouette around Atherton and sped away. As he did, the ice gave slightly under his weight, leaving a hairline crack in his wake.

Atherton opened his eyes and tried to figure out what had happened. Damien seemed to have disappeared. He turned around and saw the boy tearing off in the opposite direction. Atherton awkwardly reversed his field and began to skate after him, stumbling heavily, causing the minuscule fault in the ice to widen along his path.

The fault sped along in front of Atherton, faster than the bumbling man, until the ice started to crack under Damien.

Buher was the first to see it. Reacting quickly, he took off in the direction of the two skaters.

Suddenly, there were two very loud, very angry-sounding cracks, and the ice split wide around Atherton. The other skaters froze in place. The spectators on the shore began to cry out.

Buher finally reached Damien. He grabbed the boy around his waist, lifted him off the ice, and swung him around to safety, missing the crack by inches.

Atherton was terrified now. He could see what was happening, but he was powerless to do anything about it. He simply could not move off the fault quickly enough.

'Bill! Hold on!' Thorn cried out, and skated swiftly toward his friend.

More cracks sounded in the chilled air, cracks as sharp as the sound of cold bones breaking. The ice around Atherton snapped off into thick, floating chunks, leaving him marooned on a tiny, wobbling island in the middle of the cold, dark river.

The other skaters skidded to a halt around the periphery of the ever-widening hole, shouting out to Atherton to grab on as they held out hands and hockey sticks.

But it was useless. Atherton's weight began to tip his little island of safety, and he began to slide toward the dark and swirling current underneath the surface of the ice.

On shore, Ann put her hand over her mouth to stifle her scream. She could see what was going to happen, and there was no way to stop it.

Damien struggled to get out of Buher's grip. He wanted desperately to help, but Buher was far too strong for him, and held on fast to his body.

'Jump!' Pasarian screamed.

But it was too late. The ice floe beneath Atherton tilted forward under his weight, skidded out from underneath him, and pitched him headlong into the swift and freezing black water below.

Atherton went under completely. For a few seconds, he could not be seen. And then he suddenly bobbed up, gasping desperately, and reached with a gloved hand for the rim of the ice.

The men, led by Thorn, stretched out on their bellies on the ice and formed a chain, one man's hands holding onto the next man's ankles. Thorn shouted and held out his hand, trying to reach Atherton's fast-freezing fingers.

Atherton's head was barely above the water. His eyes were wild with fear. He pawed at the ice, trying to scramble back up to safety, but the sharp edges sliced his gloves and his hands and his wrists into ribbons. He watched his blood flow onto the shimmering icy surface of the lake.

He let out one heartbreaking wail before the current gripped him and pulled him down. He disappeared from sight.

The other skaters could not believe their eyes. They stood up, looking all around, wondering what to do next.

Suddenly, right below Thorn's feet, a face appeared, pressed flat against the under surface of the ice. It was Atherton. His eyes were open wide, pleading. His bloodied fists beat feebly at the ice. There was a scream, or what looked like a scream, before he was towed away again, kicking and clawing at the thick sheet of ice above him like a man trying to pound his way out from under a huge heavy glass wall.

For a while they were able to keep track of Atherton by the line of pink stains he left behind him under the ice.

The skaters, galvanized into desperate, futile action, raced along the surface of the lake, following the path of the freezing, drowning man. They battered the thick surface of the ice with their hockey sticks, trying to break through, trying to get to the man who floated under the ice in the water below them.

Damien finally broke free of Buher and raced to join the others. In desperation, Thorn pounded at the ice with the sharp edges of his skate blades, trying to kick his way through.

Under the ice, Atherton was beginning to suffocate. Through the thick prism of the ice above him, he could see the shadowy forms of the people trying to help him, and he could hear their muted cries. But he could not get through to them.

His lungs were bursting, beginning to fill up with icy water.

But then up ahead he thought he could make out a light, a circle of brightness in the otherwise murky water. It was a tree, growing out of the side of the riverbank, up through the ice, and into the *air*! With what little consciousness he had left, Atherton began to pray.

Miraculously, he was swept up into the opening.

Damien was the first to see him. 'There he is!' he shouted.

The skaters rushed toward the tree, skidding to a halt far enough away so that they didn't all go tumbling into the ice. Atherton's head poked up through the opening, his face hideously distorted, his mouth open and gaping like a harpooned fish as he struggled violently for air.

'We're coming!' shouted Thorn, as he and Damien inched themselves forward on the precariously thin ice. They reached out for the dying man.

Atherton's face showed for only one instant more. And then, as if a giant hand had pulled at his ankles and dragged him down under, his dark form was sucked toward the bottom of the lake and was gone.

'Spread out everybody!' cried Thorn. 'We've lost him!'

But it was a pointless pursuit. He was gone. And as the skaters formed a long line and began sweeping the length of the river again, the great black raven let out a cry and circled away into the now overcast sky.

CHAPTER FIVE

Atherton had been dead for nearly a month; Paul Buher was still redecorating his new office. He had wood paneling put over the wallpaper and had installed sharp, clean, contemporary furniture of the black-leather-and-gleaming-chrome Bauhaus style to replace Atherton's old-men's-club overstuffed leather chairs. It pleased him to have his office resemble the dining room of Thorn's Chicago apartment; after all, that was where it had all begun.

It also pleased him to have his picture put up, handsomely framed, in the outer office where his receptionist and secretary worked. The studio portrait was where it was supposed to be . . . where Atherton's had been.

But what pleased him most of all, on this January morning as he emerged from his chauffeur-driven limousine in front of the main offices of Thorn Industries, was that Byron, his bright, obsequious, and endlessly helpful young executive assistant, was waiting just inside the main doors for him in order to thrust a particular magazine into his hands.

It was the latest issue of *Fortune*, and on its cover was a copy of the same Bachrach portrait which now hung in Buher's outer office; Buher had flown to New York expressly to have it taken. The caption on the magazine cover read: PAUL BUHER, NEW PRESIDENT OF THORN INDUSTRIES.

Byron stood very still in his double-knit suit and his blow-dried hair, anxiously awaiting his boss's response.

Buher nodded slightly, acknowledging the existence

of the magazine, said, 'Thanks, Byron,' and walked quickly past him.

Byron was crestfallen. 'Oh,' he said, 'then you've already seen it.'

Buher looked at his assistant with undisguised contempt. 'You don't think these things happen by accident, do you?' He couldn't believe Byron's naïveté at times. *He* hadn't been that naïve ten years ago. At least he didn't think he had. It was hard to remember. The older Buher got, the more selective his memory became. At this point, he had nearly blanked out his childhood, and his adolescence was fading fast.

Byron interrupted his train of thought. 'I think it's neat,' he said, still referring to the cover of *Fortune*.

Buher didn't even bother to nod. Of course Byron thought it was 'neat.' He thought everything was 'neat,' with the exception of those things he thought were 'super.'

They waited for the elevator together.

'Any news of Pasarian?' Buher asked.

'No, sir,' Byron said. 'He seems to have disappeared completely.'

The elevator doors slid open, and the two men entered. Buher pressed the only button the elevator had, the one that let him out at the rear entrance to the spacious office that was now his.

Byron waited until they were perhaps three floors up before hitting Buher with his zinger for the day: 'Richard wants to see you right away.'

Buher was startled, but only for a fraction of a second. He recognized the ploy. He'd used it hundreds of times himself in his climb to the top. What Byron was trying to say was: Richard is back early from his vacation. I know it and you don't. He wants to see you. Now. That probably means you are in trouble. I referred to him as Richard. I have never called him anything but Mr Thorn before. This perhaps means that he and I are on a new level of intimacy, one that has been achieved behind your back, while you were busy redecorating your office and getting your face on the cover of *Fortune* magazine. It is possible that I may even know *why* Richard, as I know call him, is so anxious to see you.

But Byron was playing against the best. It was as though he had opened up a chess game with the Capablanca defense against Capablanca himself. 'Oh?' said Buher calmly. 'Is he in already?'

Byron was crushed. 'Yes,' he said, frowning, trying desperately to think of something else to say. He finally added, 'And he's got a great suntan too.'

As both men knew, it was a hopelessly inadequate retort.

When Buher walked in, Thorn was sipping coffee at one end of a table that could have seated an entire UN delegation. Before Buher even had a chance to say hello, Thorn snapped out at him. 'And what the *hell* is Pasarian doing in India?'

Buher set his briefcase down on the table and seated himself before answering. It gave him time to think of what he wanted to say. And to read the signs. The collar of Thorn's monogrammed Brooks Brothers shirt was open. He wore no necktie. He needed a shave. All of this was Thorn's prerogative, of course, but he would not appear in the offices of his own firm looking like this unless he had been brought back from his rest by a matter of some urgency.

Thorn wasn't just acting angry; he *was* angry.

'I needed a second opinion on some of our proposed land purchases there,' said Buher. 'Who better –?'

'Are we buying already?' Thorn asked. He was genuinely startled.

'You agreed I could activate the conclusions of my report in full,' Buher said, more defensively than he intended. 'That was a condition of my acceptance of the presidency.'

Thorn rubbed his face with both hands and sighed. 'That doesn't mean you can exclude me from the running of my own company,' he said. 'You don't activate anything without calling me first. If I didn't make that sufficiently clear before, I'm doing so now.'

'You were away on holiday,' Buher protested. 'I thought it best not to disturb you.' Even as he spoke the words, he was aware of how false the explanation sounded.

'I was always at the end of a phone,' Thorn said. Then he dropped his head onto his chest in exhaustion and added quietly, 'Bill would never have made those decisions without informing me.'

'I'm not Bill,' Buher said.

'I don't expect you to be!' said Thorn sharply. 'But I do expect you to observe the rules of company conduct!'

There was a long silence. When it became obvious that Buher had no reply to that, Thorn softened the blow a bit. 'Paul,' he said, 'you're as brilliant as they come. You deserve to be at the top. But don't screw it up for yourself. Don't *ever* forget whose company this is.'

'It won't happen again.' Buher sounded sincerely penitent. He waited silently until he felt enough time had passed, and then he tried changing the subject. 'You were looking for Pasarian,' he said. 'Why?'

'Something's wrong with his design of the P-84 unit,' Thorn said. 'Walker's getting very agitated about it.' With that one sentence, his entire manner had changed, just as Buher had hoped it would. The bone of contention had been discussed, and Thorn had made himself eminently clear. Now the issue was past. It would never be discussed again unless, or until, Buher made the same transgression. And if he did, then the axe would fall, and no explanation would be necessary.

'I know Walker's always doom and disaster,' Thorn went on, 'but this time he's got *me* going.'

'I'll take care of it, Richard,' Buher said, getting up to leave. He could sense that the meeting was over.

'See that you do,' Thorn said. He waited until Buher had left the room before standing up and walking over to the large window that looked down on the elegant old Water Tower in midtown Chicago. The view usually afforded him some kind of comfort, but on this particular morning it didn't. Thorn was far too upset.

Something had been gnawing away at him since the tragedy of Atherton's death, but just what it was, he had no idea. No sooner did his mind get a hold of the idea, than it skittered away again, out of reach.

CHAPTER SIX

The course was entitled 'Military History: Theories and Practice.' It sounded more interesting than it actually was, being little more than a fairly sketchy survey of the most famous battles of the past. But the idea was to instill in the cadets at Davidson a healthy respect for the glory of war. Sometimes it worked; most times it didn't. But the course was required, so everyone had to take it.

Today, the Military History class, which included most of the members of Neff's platoon, was learning about Attila the Hun. The instructor, a tall, stringy man with straight black hair parted down the middle, was also the school chaplain. He taught wearing a tight clerical collar and a tweed jacket. His name was Budman.

Chaplain Budman had a deep personal interest in Attila, just as other people have in beloved authors or composers. When he read accounts of Attila's life and exploits, Chaplain Budman felt he could see beyond the cold pages of history and into the soul of the man who had done those deeds. And what he thought he found was a deeply misunderstood man, a martyr, a man, in fact, not unlike himself.

'The poor man,' Chaplain Budman was saying, 'is, of course, badly misinterpreted by history. You have to understand that Attila was considered a just ruler by his own people . . .'

Damien was the only one who was listening, which was odd since he had never done well in history, had indeed always felt some strange resistance to it. But over the past couple of months, he had found himself becoming more and more fascinated by the details of those who had lived and died many years ago.

'He was far less concerned with devastation,' the chaplain continued, 'than many of the conquerors before him or after him . . .'

Mark was having a good time with Teddy, who now made a point of sitting with the Thorns in class. Mark had just finished scribbling something on a piece of paper, and Teddy was doing everything he could to keep from giggling.

'In fact,' said Chaplain Budman, 'Attila was so keen on being educated that he invited many learned Romans into his court . . .'

Just then, Mark showed his piece of paper to Damien who, caught totally by surprise, immediately burst out laughing.

The chaplain stopped in mid-sentence. 'Who laughed?' he asked.

Damien stood up immediately. 'I did, Chaplain,' he said.

'Come here,' said Budman, 'and bring that piece of paper with you.'

Damien did as he was told.

Mark squirmed uneasily in his seat, feeling guilty. Teddy kicked him in the shins. 'Chicken!' he whispered.

The other students watched with that vague combination of pleasure and fear that arises any time a teacher and a fellow student collide.

Chaplain Budman took the piece of paper from Damien's hand. It was a drawing of himself, quite a good one in fact, wearing his clerical collar and riding on horseback, holding aloft the severed head of a slain Mongol enemy.

The chaplain was mortified. Not only was *he* being made fun of, but his revered Attila was still being

113

maligned, even as he spoke, and by the most intelligent of his students at that. Or so he thought.

Budman crumpled up the drawing and threw it in the wastebasket by his desk. 'So,' he said, after a dramatic and properly fear-inducing pause, 'we have an artist in the class. What's wrong, Thorn, am I boring you?' He didn't even give Damien a chance to answer, but continued with heavy sarcasm, 'You, of course, know all about Attila's campaigns.'

Taking a deep breath, Damien replied, 'Something about them, sir.' Damien was as surprised as anyone else in the room at his reply.

' "Something" about them, eh?' the chaplain repeated, with the same heavy sarcasm. 'If Attila had known only "something" about warfare, instead of everything about it, we wouldn't even know his name today.' He paused and narrowed his eyes. 'Do you know anything beyond his name, Thorn? Do you know anything about him and the Romans, for example?'

Damien took another deep breath. 'I think I do, sir.' He knew nothing! What the hell was he doing?

The class murmured among themselves, wondering what Damien was letting himself in for. Direct confrontation was not his style.

'You "think" you do,' the chaplain said. 'Well, let's find out, shall we? Tell me, Thorn, what was the size of Attila's army when he invaded Gaul?'

'Approximately half a million men, sir,' said Damien, and before he had time to even wonder how he had known the answer, he heard himself saying, 'But he was defeated in the Battle of Châlons by Aetius in 451. He then turned back, invading northern Italy, but did not go on to Rome.'

Budman was taken aback. He hadn't expected this. But he couldn't back down now, not in front of the class. He had started this thing and would have to see it through.

In any case, it sounded to him like a quotation from the encyclopedia. Maybe Thorn was one of those students who knew everything by rote, who could tell you that Columbus discovered America in 1492, but who had no idea why Columbus was in the Indies in the first place, or what he was looking for.

Budman decided to try what, in an exam, would have been called an essay question. 'Why not?' he asked.

Again, Damien didn't hesitate for an instant. 'The credit,' he said, 'usually goes to Pope Leo I, for his diplomatic skill. But the real reason was lack of provisions —' Here Damien hesitated, and for a moment Budman thought the boy was stumped. But in his mind's eye, Damien had come up against the ugly vision of venereal disease, and he was simply trying to find the most diplomatic way to explain it. Finally he said, 'And the Army came down with, uh . . . a pestilence.'

A few of the cadets caught the meaning, tact or no tact, and snickered. Damien blushed.

The chaplain was furious. 'Quiet!' he shouted at the class. Then, turning back to Damien, he decided he'd better trip the boy up on hard facts and get this embarrassing confrontation over with.

'What was Attila's date of birth?'

'Unknown, sir,' Damien said.

'Date of rule?'

'From 445 to 453 A.D., sir. He died of a nasal hemorrhage while . . . uh . . . celebrating his last marriage.'

This time the entire class broke up.

'Shut up!' the chaplain screamed, his self-esteem shaken. He moved closer to Damien and said, directly into the boy's face, as if daring him to answer, 'What was his brother's name?'

'Bleda,' Damien said, but again he didn't stop with the simple answer. Suddenly, he burned with the bright, fierce light of a knowledge he hadn't even known he possessed. His eyes glowed. The power of his presence

115

blazed and pulsated visibly in the tiny classroom. Damien knew, and yet he did not know *how* he knew, everything there was to know about Attila the Hun. And not just the facts, either. He was as though he could see inside Attila's head. He knew his thoughts, his dreams, his wildest fantasies, and he was as certain they were true as if they'd been his own. It was as though he had known Attila in a previous life.

Or, perhaps, *been* him.

'Attila and his brother Bleda inherited the Hun empire in 434 A.D.,' Damien went on. 'It extended from the Alps and the Baltic to the Caspian Sea.' He spread his arms wide like an emperor. 'The two brothers were inseparable,' Damien continued, fixing his eyes on Mark. The power of his gaze made Mark shiver involuntarily. 'Between the years 435 and 439, although there aren't any records of it, it's assumed Attila subdued the barbarians in the northern and eastern ends of his empire.' He stopped and looked at Budman. 'Shall I go on?' he asked.

But there was no stopping Damien now, and the chaplain knew it. He was both amazed and terrified by the boy, but something told him to let the scene play out. He nodded for Damien to go on.

And so he did. 'In 441,' Damien said, 'the Roman Empire neglected to pay Attila his proper tributes, and he assaulted the Danubian frontier. He was a magnificent warrior and there was simply no standing against him. A year later, the Romans arranged a truce.'

The class was mesmerized.

'And Attila was a clever politician as well,' Damien said. 'He knew how to turn the superstitions of his people to his advantage. For instance, the Scythians worshipped the bare sword as a god, even though this god was supposed to have disappeared from the earth.

'One day,' Damien continued, 'a herdsman who was tracking a lost heifer in the desert stumbled over a

116

sword that was sticking up in the sand as though it had
been thrown down from heaven. He brought it to Attila,
who then apeared before his armies holding the sword
up in the air, declaring that he wielded the spirit of
Death-in-Battle.'

The class hung on his every word. Mark, however,
was gradually and inexplicably becoming terrified.

And now Damien said something that even the
chaplain had never heard: 'It's possible,' he said, 'that
Attila held the sword up in the air like that because
it reminded him of his childhood. Attila had been held
up like that himself. His mother believed that if she
held him up to the sun for an hour every day, he would
become invested with the sun's power. Some say this
changed the pigment in his skin, accounting for his
swarthy appearance.' Damien stopped to catch his
breath. His heart was pounding wildly against the wall
of his chest. 'That happened when he was three.'

The chaplain simply gaped at him.

But Damien knew still more. Some other power was
forcing the facts out of him. 'Attila bore little resem-
blance to his brother,' he went on, 'skin pigmentation
aside. But then his mother was known to have enter-
tained quite a few men in her time, and openly at
that.

'In his first battle, he was about my age.' He quickly
corrected himself. 'Our age, I mean. There is a painting
that shows him at that age with his sword seeming to
impale three different men at once. Probably an exag-
geration. He was also very handsome at that age, and
desired by many women. Not long after that, he began
to participate in black masses.'

That was too much for Budman. 'That's outrageous!'
he said. 'Where did you find that information? *Name
your source!*' It was a favourite command of Budman's.

Damien faltered for the first time. 'I . . . I don't
know, sir.' Suddenly, he seemed confused, bewildered,

117

unsure of himself, as if he had crossed over into unfamiliar territory.

The chaplain seized the advantage. 'And his brother – I suppose *he* participated in these black masses, too, eh?'

'Oh, no, sir,' Damien said, shaking his head with complete conviction and authority. 'By that time Attila had killed him.'

Mark gasped.

By now, Damien, couldn't even comprehend the meaning of what he was saying. The words just kept pouring out, as if of their own volition. 'He had to, in order to rule alone.' Damien made it sound as though there had been no alternative. 'And then,' he said, lowering his voice as if to share a great, dark secret, 'he started calling himself names like the Great Nimrod, the Scourge of God, and . . . the *Anti-Christ*!'

The classroom was dead silent.

Just then, the door burst open and Neff strode in. He walked straight over to the chaplain, who by now was sweating and shaking, in a state of near disintegration, and whispered a few words to him. The chaplain nodded.

Neff turned to Damien. 'Come with me, Thorn,' he said.

Without a word, Damien did as he was told.

'Copy what's on the blackboard,' Chaplain Budman shot at the astonished class and followed Damien and Neff, leaving a deathly silence behind him. Then the class suddenly broke into a furious, speculative chatter.

Neff walked Damien down the hall, far enough away so that they could not be heard by anyone. Behind them, the chaplain brushed past on his way to the men's room, badly in need of a drink of water. When the door swung closed, Neff turned to the boy and said angrily, 'What were you trying to do in there, Damien?' It was the first time he had ever called him by his first name.

Still overwhelmed and bewildered by his own performance, Damien said, 'I was just answering questions, Sergeant.'

Neff shook his head. 'You were showing off,' he said.

Damien didn't even stop to wonder how Neff could have known what had happened. He was too full of what he had done, what he had never realized was in his own *power* to do. 'But I knew all the answers!' he tried to explain. 'Somehow, I just knew them all!'

Neff was stern. 'You mustn't attract attention,' he said.

'I wasn't trying to,' protested Damien. 'I just felt this –'

Neff cut through Damien's reply: 'The day will come,' he said, 'when everyone will know who you are, but that day is not yet here.'

It was just what Buher had said.

Confused, Damien asked, 'Who *am* I?' He was beginning to get frightened. He didn't know what was going on, what he was destined for, why all these men seemed to be singling him out. He thought he must be going crazy.

'Read your Bible,' Neff said. 'In the New Testament there is the Book of Revelation. For you, Damien, it is just that . . . a Book of Revelation . . . for *you* . . . *about* you.'

Damien stared at him.

'Read it,' Neff said with terrible urgency. 'Read, learn, understand.'

Damien started to cry out of fear and frustration. 'What am I supposed to understand?' he asked, holding his hands out in supplication. 'Please *tell* me!'

Neff stared at the boy a long time before he answered. Then, in a quiet, infinitely respectful voice, he said, 'Who you are.' And he seemed to bow before he walked away.

Damien stood in the dark and echoing hallway, with

119

tears streaming down his face, trying to put all the pieces together, trying to figure out what all these people were saying to him. Finally he decided to seek out the Book of Revelation to see what was written there.

And if it was, indeed, about himself.

CHAPTER SEVEN

Davidson Military Academy had quite a good band, whose main function was to play at their sporting events and other celebrations. Mark was head bugler. Though the bugle has a limited range of notes, Mark was amazingly adept at drawing great expression out of it. He had the task – which he considered an honor – of blowing all the bugle calls at the school. He didn't mind having to get up a half hour early to play 'Reveille' over the school loudspeaker system, and, surprisingly, the boys seemed to mind being awakened a little less when Mark was doing the playing. Nor did they mind when Mark's sensitive playing of 'Taps' told them it was time to put out the lights and go to bed.

They positively loved Mark's rendition of 'Mess Call,' even when it heralded a meatless day and the cook, rumored to have served under Robert E. Lee in the Civil War, trotted out one of his unpalatable noodle-and-cheese dishes or tasteless tuna fish casseroles. On those occasions, Mark gave 'Mess Call' an extra 'oomph,' as though he were playing a vamp number for a striptease dancer.

Today, because it looked like rain, the band was practicing its parade drill indoors. The boys' dormitory had been built to accommodate indoor activities. The small cell-like rooms were all on the second floor, which ran like a wide balcony all the way around the building, overlooking the parade area below. The classrooms were on the first floor, directly under the bedrooms. So what was left below was a wide-open central space with plenty of room, below a two-story-high ceiling, to rehearse the complicated formations the parade band made as they marched.

The band was playing Sousa's 'The Thunderer' now, a march Mark loved. He was in seventh heaven as he stepped about smartly and precisely, letting the music wash over him, the snare drums in cadence with his pulse. Because of the accoustics, indoor rehearsal was definitely more exciting.

Even though it was still early afternoon, it was beginning to get dark outside. Those students who were not in the band were either studying in their rooms or working out in the gym. It was the free period of the day.

No one noticed Damien, who was engaged in a larcenous act. He had just stolen Chaplain Budman's Bible.

There were no Bibles in the boys' rooms. The school might have thought to provide them with books on football plays, but not with the Word of God. And the long arm of Gideon did not reach as far as Davidson. The first place Damien had gone to look for a Bible was the library, which seemed the most logical place to start. But he had been unable to locate one even there. He assumed he was working in the wrong stacks or under the wrong titles in the card index, but he was much too cautious to ask for help. He wanted no one to know.

But, being an intelligent and resourceful boy, he realized that the staff member most likely to have a copy of the Bible in his office was, of course, the chaplain. It was simply a matter of finding it.

And so he waited until the midafternoon break when most cadets and staff retired to their rooms, and when the band would be making lots of noise. Then he stole into the chaplain's office, which, in keeping with the honor system at Davidson, was never locked.

There were several copies of the King James version of

the Bible on the shelf behind Budman's desk. Damien took the drabbest-looking volume hoping it would be the one least likely to be missed. He was counting on reading it that afternoon and having it back the same night.

As he moved along the balcony toward his room, the blood was racing through his veins. He shoved aside the curtain that took the place of a door to his room ('A fella who needs a lock is a fella with something to hide,' the Colonel liked to say) and sat down to collect himself. He held his head in his hands to keep it from spinning with the dizziness and excitement of the moment.

He was about to find out who he was.

It was a terrifying prospect. How many people, if told a particular book held the answer to the riddle of their existence, would have the courage to open its pages?

Damien, for one, did. Tearing the blanket and sheets off his bed and piling them below the curtained door to block out the light that was evidence of his presence, he pulled the stolen Bible from under his military tunic, stretched himself full-length on his taut belly on the bare mattress, and set the book on the floor, where the light from the single tensor lamp would best hit it. He opened the Bible to the Book of Revelation and began to read.

> And all the world wondered after the Beast. And they worshipped the dragon which gave power unto the Beast. And they worshipped the Beast, saying, 'Who is like unto the Beast? Who is able to make war with him?'

Damien looked up from the book and tried to think what that meant. He thought about Mark, who had always seemed to worship him from the start, and about how Teddy did now. And he thought about Buher and Neff, and how they had singled him out and made him

123

feel special and more important than even *they* were. And he thought about his athletic ability, and how no one seemed able to beat him at anything.

Excitedly, he read on:

> And I saw the Beast, and the kings of the earth, and their armies, gathered together to make war against him that sat on the horse, and against his army . . .

And he remembered how clearly he had understood Attila, and how, as he had talked, the images had become so startlingly clear that it was as if he were there, astride a horse, surrounded by a horde of warriors awaiting his evil command.

He swallowed hard. The feeling growing inside him was about to explode. He pushed himself up off the bed and began to pace around. He had to move, he had to act. Although his fear was great, his hunger to learn more was even greater. He leaned down and scooped the book up off the floor in one swift motion; with burning eyes, he lifted it up and read:

> And the Beast which I saw was like unto a leopard, and his feet were as the feet of a bear, and his mouth as the mouth of a lion; and the dragon gave him his power, and his seat, and great authority.

Damien understood that the words were metaphors, and knew somehow that Attila had often been described that way. His soldiers would come back from battle and tell stories of how fierce he had been, and what he had looked like as he fought. And Damien thought about how the stories must have grown with each retelling, until they had become legend, and how Attila had become an awesome, composite beast against whom no man could hope to stand.

He wondered if people would ever tell tales like that about him. And then he read on:

> And through his policy also shall he cause craft to prosper in his hand, and he shall magnify himself in his heart, and by peace shall destroy many; he shall also stand up against the Prince of Princes.

('You should know all about the Thorn holdings,' Buher had told him. 'After all, they'll be yours one day.')

But to go up against the Prince of Princes? Even in the first full rush of his power, Damien's initial thought was, But I can't! I'm just a kid!

Now he began to be aware of the dreadful responsibility that would be his, even though he had not asked for it, and his legs began to tremble with fear. He no longer wanted this gift that had made him so potent in the classroom. It had become a burden, like a huge boulder pressing down on his back, and he longed for the strength to be able to cast it away.

He felt compelled to read on, although the words swam before his eyes, which were suddenly moist:

> And he causeth all, both small and great, rich and poor, free and bond, to receive a mark in their right hand, or in their foreheads: And that no man might buy or sell, save that he had the mark, or the name of the Beast, or the number of his name. And it was given unto him to make war with the saints, *and to overcome them*: and power was given him over all kindreds and tongues, and nations!

Damien's heart was beating wildly. What he wanted now more than anything in all the world was to stop reading, to forget what he had just read, to take the foul book back, to throw it away, to burn it.

He hurled the Bible across the room. It bounced against the opposite wall, and landed on the floor. The cadet in the next room pounded on the wall for quiet.

Damien stood very, very still and stared at the book. It drew him like a fire. Although he felt it would burn him if he touched it, it was so alluring, so tantalizing, he could not help himself. He knew he was only inches away from the heart of the mystery, and he had to know what came next, even if it cost him his soul.

He picked up the book gingerly, and opened once again to the Book of Revelation. The pages were bent and crumpled where the open book had hit the wall.

A shudder ran through his body like a fever. His hands trembled as he found the place where he had stopped reading, and, with the greatest effort of will he had ever made in his life, he read on:

> Here is wisdom. Let him that hath understanding count the number of the Beast: for it is the number of a man; and his number is six hundred threescore and six.

Damien slammed the book shut. So there *was* proof, a mark! And if he didn't have it, he would be safe and free! Clutching the Bible to his chest, although he loathed it and would have liked to tear it apart page by page, he rushed out of the room, kicking aside his sheets-and-blankets barricade. Not caring who saw him now, he rushed down the hall to the washroom.

No one was in the lavatory. The tiles gleamed in the fluorescent light, brighter than the day outside, which had grown ever darker. The wind had picked up and was howling through the treetops, pushing dark clouds across the sky.

With trembling hands, Damien set the stolen Bible

down on the sink and stood before the toothpaste-spattered mirror. There was no doubt in his mind as to what he was looking for. He rubbed a section clean with the heel of his hand, then peered closely at the reflection.

There was no mark on his right hand, that was obvious. He would have seen it a thousand times. Even so, he checked once more, subjecting his hand to the most intense scrutiny under the fluorescent tube.

Nothing. A normal hand. Then it occurred to him that there was another place it might be where he might never have noticed it.

He parted his hair with shaking hands and looked.

Nothing.

He parted his hair again, in another spot, and looked.

Still nothing. He began to think he was going mad. Why else would he allow himself even to imagine the possibility of this horror?

Or was it just that he was letting the grown-ups instill their own fears in *him*? Now that he was thirteen and supposedly a man, maybe he was feeling the first stirrings of the sexual urge. Maybe this was what sex was. Maybe this was why it made some people go crazy.

Another boy, having seen what he had hoped to see, but was afraid he would not (or rather, having *not* seen what he feared he would), might have stopped there.

But not Damien; whatever else he was, he believed he was a Thorn, and the Thorns were thorough. He had been taught to be that for as long as he could remember.

This time Damien reached high up onto his forehead and spread his hair apart once again.

And there it was.

No wonder no one had ever seen it. It was so *tiny*. But it was there. Or *they* were there, to be more exact; a tiny cluster of sixes, barely noticeable even under the powerful light of the fluorescent bulb overhead.

666.

Damien gasped, and stumbled back against the wall with the enormity of the shock. It was true – everything he had feared, everything Neff had told him, everything Buher had slyly hinted at. It was *all true*.

And he was only a young boy.

Tears sprang to his eyes as he bolted out of the lavatory, clutching the Bible to his chest. He didn't know what to do, where to go. All he knew was that he needed to be alone for a while.

He ran along the balcony and headed for the stairs. The band was still there, practicing. As Damien tore down the stairs and broke through the ranks on his way out, Mark caught sight of him and called out, 'Damien!'

But Damien kept on going. As he passed by Chaplain Budman's office, he stopped to return the Bible. But the chaplain's door was ajar now. That meant he was there. Damien tossed the Bible onto the floor in the hallway outside Budman's office. Then he took off in the opposite direction. He ran down the hall and out of the building, out across the abandoned athletic field, beyond that to the gated entrance to the Academy, past that, and down the road, running, running, running as he had never run before, running away, trying to get away from the school, from Neff, and Buher, and the Bible, and the terrible knowledge of what he was.

Trying to run away from himself.

Damien kept on going down the road until his lungs pumped fire with every breath and his legs were lead and felt as though he could not possibly lift them one more time.

When it seemed he might die if he took another step, he staggered up to a lone tree and knelt down against it and wept.

After a long moment, he looked up at the darkening sky, filled up with rain clouds and the sound of thunder. He stretched out his arms in a passionate protest. Or was it surrender?

Then he broke down again, sobbing despairingly.

Above him, high in the top of the tree, sat the enormous black raven. It cocked its head knowingly and stared down at the stricken boy far below with something akin to triumph in its eyes.

Damien would have been shocked, although he would also have understood, had he been there to witness either one of two small miracles that occurred that night.

The first took place in Paul Buher's bedroom as Buher got ready for bed. He took off the ring that he had worn on the fourth finger of his right hand from the moment he had been 'called,' and there on his finger was the mark he had been awaiting, all this time. It was tiny, barely noticeable. Buher was rapturous. He had received the sign. The three figures – 666. He had been accepted at last.

The second took place in the small bathroom of Daniel Neff's tiny faculty apartment. After he washed his face and brushed his teeth, he pushed back the hair on his forehead and leaned in toward the mirror to look, as he had done every night since the 'calling' had come. And tonight the mark was there. Finally. Three figures – 666.

Nothing stood in their way.

It was shortly after ten o'clock. Mark stirred in a sleep that was really no sleep at all.

He had returned after band practice to the room he shared with Damien and found the tangled bedding on the floor. He had remade his foster brother's bed, and now he lay on his own bunk, with the tensor light on low, worrying and waiting, trying to rest. He didn't know what was wrong. He had seen Damien go berserk in class that day and then run out of the building later on, but they hadn't had a chance to talk, and Damien was still not back yet. Mark was afraid and couldn't sleep.

Finally he heard Damien's light footfall. He rolled over and looked up to find Damien standing just inside the doorway, looking down at him.

'Where've you been?' Mark asked, genuinely concerned. 'I've been worried!'

Damien said nothing. He moved silent to his bunk and lay down on it, staring up at the ceiling, not even acknowledging the fact that Mark had made it up for him from the mess he had left on the floor.

'Damien!' Mark whispered urgently, but he got no answer. He watched Damien stare at the ceiling until he could stand it no longer, and whispered, even more loudly, 'Are you all right?'

For a long time, Damien didn't respond. Then he finally said: 'I'm okay now. Put out the light. You'll get us in trouble.'

Mark did as he was told. For a moment, the room was completely dark and totally silent. When his eyes had readjusted to the darkness, and he could see Damien still lying there, staring at the ceiling, Mark asked, 'You sure you're okay?'

'Go to sleep,' Damien said, his voice unusually harsh and stiff. And he rolled over and went to sleep himself.

But it was a long time before Mark did.

CHAPTER EIGHT

Pasarian, exhausted from jet lag and lugging a bulging briefcase, ran across the tarmac. Behind him, the largest Thorn Industries jet was beginning to cool down after its nonstop flight from India.

Pasarian went straight for the nearest pay phone. Although it was late Sunday evening, the call could not wait. Thorn had to be told what had happened. Immediately.

Fortunately, Pasarian had access to a company credit card number; he had nothing but Indian coins with him. Tapping nervously against the glass of the phone booth, he waited for a call to be put through to the Thorns' lakeside retreat.

The butler who answered the phone told him that Thorn would be out late that evening and could not be reached, but he assured Pasarian that the message would be conveyed to Thorn in the morning.

Disappointed, Pasarian debated what he should do next. If he waited until morning, things could only get worse. And yet Thorn was really the only one who should be told. Pasarian thought for a while, then made his decision. Against his better judgment, he picked up the phone and put in a call to Buher.

Buher's apartment was as sparse and impersonal, as coldly formal, as the reception area of a new bank. The only remarkable thing about it was the view, a breathtaking panorama of Chicago. The rest of the place seemed to have been designed solely for efficiency, everything personal or homelike had been sacrificed.

Buher had been reading when the phone rang. Because he had had the phones in his apartment installed in such a way that, no matter where he was, he wouldn't have to get up, he simply reached over and picked up the closest receiver.

'Buher,' he said.

There was a pause, a moment's hesitation, then Pasarian's voice came on the line. 'Paul? It's me, David. I have to talk to you.'

'Where are you?' Buher's voice tightened with concern.

'At the airport. Here in Chicago. I had to leave early. There's been trouble.'

Buher cut him off. 'You'd better get over here right away.'

At that very moment, Richard and Ann were enjoying an evening together. With the boys back at school, no guests around to entertain, no meetings to dash off to, and no telephone calls to make, they were feeling especially relaxed and romantic, and had decided to take a late-night sleigh ride through the snow.

The sleigh was a big, old-fashioned one, so heavy that the only kind of horse that could pull it with any ease or speed was a Clydesdale. The Christmas before, Richard had bought a pair of Clydesdales from a friend in the Busch beer family. Ann had been in charge of retouching the paint job on the sleigh and outfitting it with bells. Tonight, they were headed back home, after a fast and exhilarating run through the snow. The sound of the bells, the horse's hooves, and the rushing of the sleigh's runners through the snow signaled the approach of the vehicle long before it came into view. Inside its magic enclosure, Ann and Richard sat very close together, bundled under the same warm blanket,

132

and wondered what they had done to deserve so much, and to be so happy . . .

Richard found the message from Pasarian as soon as he walked in the front door. He tried calling him immediately, but Pasarian was not at home. Richard shrugged and hung up. 'Not there,' he said, turning to Ann and taking her in his arms. 'I'll see him tomorrow. It can't be that important.'

Ann, fresh-faced and lovely, with tiny flakes of snow still in her hair, reached up and kissed him. '*Nothing's* more important than what I've got in store for you . . .' she murmured.

Richard returned her kiss, long and lingeringly, and then Ann took him by the hand and led him upstairs to their bedroom.

An exhausted and distracted Pasarian sat on a black leather-and-chrome Mies van der Rohe couch in Buher's austerely elegant living room, and slowly sipped a cup of coffee. He had refused the drink Buher had offered because he was sure it would put him to sleep.

Buher stood nursing a drink, and staring out the window. He was trying to absorb everything that Pasarian had just told him.

'So you think,' Buher began, 'that because this man wouldn't sell to us, he was *murdered*? By one of our own people?' He downed his drink.

Pasarian nodded wearily. 'I'm almost sure of it,' he said.

'That's impossible!' said Buher, moving over to the bar to fix himself another drink.

'I was in eight provinces checking out land for us,' Pasarian said, 'and in three of them –'

'Three?'

'Three killings.' Pasarian took another sip of coffee,

then put the cup down. 'That's three too many in my book, Paul,' he said.

'Who could it be?' Buher asked, moving back to the window.

'No idea,' said Pasarian.

'Well,' said Buher, letting out a big sigh, 'I'd better look into it.'

Pasarian stood up to go. 'Shall we tell Richard?' he asked, reaching for his coat.

'We have to!' Buher said vehemently. 'I'll call him first thing tomorrow.' He helped Pasarian on with his coat. 'Oh, by the way,' he said casually 'he wants to see you.'

'Richard? What for?'

Buher walked him to the door. 'Apparently your P.84 is acting up. There's a report on your desk. Richard is worried. It's urgent you check it out in the morning.' He shook hands with Pasarian, then added, 'I don't want to have to shut it down, David.'

Pasarian nodded. 'I'll attend to it,' he said, and opened the door.

Just before they said good-night. Buher's eyes took on a peculiarly distant look as he turned to gaze out at the Chicago skyline framed by the large window. 'I hope we haven't got some overenthusiastic men in the field,' he said quietly. Then he glanced quickly back to Pasarian and smiled. 'Thanks for coming over tonight, David. I really appreciate your confidence.'

Pasarian nodded and shook hands, but he left feeling very uneasy, and wondering whether he'd just done the wrong thing.

What with Pasarian's sudden and unexpected return and the bad news that he had brought with him, and with Thorn yet to be told, and the P.84 acting up, Buher had totally forgotten that today was the day

134

that the boys from the Academy were coming to visit the immense new agricultural plant which Thorn Industries had only recently acquired.

Thus, when he happened to look out the window of his new office and saw the Davidson Military Academy bus pull up in front of the building, Buher was at first surprised, and then, when he realized why the bus was there, he buzzed his secretary and told her to hold all calls for a while. He would have to go welcome the boys.

They could hardly have chosen a more inopportune time, Buher thought. But if he couldn't handle little crises like this when they came along, then he didn't deserve to be sitting in this chair, in this office.

Outside, in the parking lot, the boys were busy being impressed. They had understood vaguely that the Thorn boys were very rich, but seeing these vast brick buildings, covering an area almost as large as the towns some of them had grown up in, was pretty overwhelming. One of them let out a long, low whistle.

Teddy decided to lighten the awestruck atmosphere. 'Does this tour include lunch in the executive dining room?' he asked, rubbing his stomach and licking his lips like some grotesque cartoon character.

'Of course,' Damien said, polite as ever.

But Mark wouldn't let Teddy get away with it. 'We're going to try out a new pesticide on you,' he said, and everyone laughed.

They moved into the main building where Buher was waiting to welcome them. Today Damien found himself a little shy with Buher. The boy had not had enough time to assimilate a *hundredth* of what he had just learned about himself. He felt stronger, though, and infinitely braver, but he knew it was still too early to act. He glanced briefly at Buher before moving over to a glass wall labeled:

PESTICIDE ROOM. NO ADMITTANCE. AUTHORIZED PERSONNEL ONLY.

135

Peering through the glass, Damien saw an enormous room, approximately the size of a basketball court. Other than one man, whom Damien recognized as Pasarian, it contained miles and miles of pipes and valves in vivid colors and intricate cross-hatchings. It looked like the intestinal system of a very large and very complicated robot.

The colors were, of course, a code, and a trained technician read the information as easily as the average person reads a newspaper. This was Pasarian's room. He had built it, and it was his baby. And it was here that they were now trying to perfect his beloved P.84.

Pasarian was standing at a large computer console, watching the dials flash out their vital information. As he did so, he punched out numbers on the push-button phone at his side.

He raised the phone to his ear and shouted to an assistant on a catwalk above him, 'Give it another hundred pounds, Tom!' Then turning back to the phone he said, 'This is Pasarian. Has Mr Thorn come in yet?'

The voice on the other end crackled, 'No, sir.'

Pasarian began to get agitated. 'He still hasn't called?'

'No, sir, he hasn't.'

'Please let me know as soon as he arrives,' Pasarian said. 'It's most urgent.' As he hung up, he swore under his breath. He checked the dials again and called out, 'Make it another fifty, Tom!'

After Buher had introduced the boys to their guide for the day, he hurried back to his office for an important meeting with all of the young up-and-coming Thorn executives. The conference had been scheduled for weeks. Buher enjoyed speaking to the new blood in the company. It gave him the chance to disseminate his ideas to those who might have the hunger and the

136

energy to help him carry them out. And it never hurt to build a kind of fan club for yourself among those who could someday be after your job.

It never failed to amaze Buher how young they looked, in their identical haircuts and three-piece suits. He always felt he might as well be delivering a commencement address to a class of Harvard Business School graduates.

'But in the case of a land acquisition project such as the one we're now arranging in India,' Buher was saying, 'we have to guard against the indigenous population thinking we are in the business of exploitation. We are *not*! Emphasize that wherever you go. We are there to *help*! These people, through no fault of their own, lack the cultural and educational advantages we here in America take for granted. We would be remiss in our duties as members of Thorn Industries, and as Americans' – Buher felt he had named those two loyalties in the proper order – 'if we did not share our bounty with those less fortunate than ourselves. And remember this: by supplying India and the Middle East with food, for example, we prevent the Russians from moving in to give them that food. Thus we gain not only their gratitude, but also their resources.'

Buher was just getting warmed up to the topic when his secretary stepped into the room. Seeing her, he paused in the middle of his speech and motioned her to speak.

'Mr Pasarian has begun working on the P.84,' she said, blushing in front of all the new young male executives. 'You asked me to let you know when he started.'

'Thank you,' said Buher, effectively dismissing her from the room. He turned to his audience and smiled graciously. 'Gentlemen,' he said, 'take a half-hour break.'

He left, closing the door behind him. The new

recruits could wait. The business with Pasarian could not.

The authorized guide showing the cadets around the plant was a well-intentioned young man from the lower echelons of the Public Relations Department. He was really giving it his all this morning, hoping his performance would impress Richard Thorn's two young sons and that they would mention him favorably to their father.

He had just taken them into the pesticide section. 'To make crops grow faster and fatter,' he was saying, 'you need more powerful and improved fertilizers, and new and innovative pesticides as well.'

The group stopped before the bolted doors of the Pesticide Room where Pasarian was working on the P.84. The guide produced the proper identifying papers for himself and then slipped the guard a twenty-dollar bill. This room was not included on the regular tour, but the guide wanted to do something special for the Thorn boys and their friends. The massive doors swung open and the cadets were taken inside. The doors were immediately pushed shut again and locked.

Once inside, the guide had to raise his voice quite a bit in order to be heard over the hum of the computers.

'This complex operation,' he practically shouted, 'is run entirely by three men at the controls of that computer over there.' He pointed in the direction of a glassed-in area halfway down the room. 'That's why you see no one here.'

Most of the boys were awestruck, all but Teddy, whose mind remained stuck in its usual groove. 'Isn't there a pesticide that works on sex?' he asked.

'Jesus, Teddy,' one of the other cadets said, 'what a one-track mind!'

But the guide defended him. 'He's absolutely right,' he said. 'Sex attractants – pheromones – are extracted

138

from insects of one sex, and put in a trap to lure in insects of the opposite sex so they can be killed. If you kill enough of just one sex of a given species, you've in effect destroyed the species itself. There's no one left to reproduce with.'

However, that information paled alongside the sheer enormity of what the boys were seeing. The guide took them up a metal stairway to a catwalk high above the maze of colored pipes.

'This is a shunting device,' the guide continued to shout as they walked, 'computerized, like everything else. It's programmed to deliver precise mixes of grasses and solutions from storage vats into the main plant.'

They would now see Pasarian working down below them on a complicated pressure gauge attached to a yellow-colored pipe connection. He happened to look up just then and recognized his two young friends. 'Mark! Damien!' he called out. 'What are you doing here?' He was alarmed that they were in this room at all, much less on a day when things were not working quite right.

The boys looked down at him, twenty feet below, and smiled. 'We're taking the grand tour!' shouted Damien. Then both he and Mark waved and moved on, leaving Pasarian puzzled and concerned.

Just then, on the far side of the room, on one of the upper levels, a pipe suddenly broke lose, and a thick, greenish vapor started hissing out into the room.

'There's a leak!' someone yelled.

Pasarian looked up in time to see his assistant, his face already blistered from the inhalation of the noxious gas, collapse and fall over the side of the railing, smashing his head on the floor below.

Pasarian could not believe it was happening. He ran back to the console, shouting 'Everybody out! Get those kids out of here!'

His voice reached up to the group of cadets and their

139

guide, who turned around, startled. The gas was already beginning to rise in their direction.

Down below, Pasarian was looking at the gauges on his console. The pressure was dropping rapidly in synchronization with the escaping gas.

There was an emergency button on the console, which might as well have been called the panic button. Pasarian pressed it as hard as he could.

He looked through the glass windows that gave onto the adjoining computer room and saw two white-coated technicians engaged in casual conversation. For some reason, the panic button was not registering. He had no way of knowing, of course, that his own superior, Buher, had adjusted the button earlier that day.

He punched the button again, but the two technicians continued to talk. Obviously, they heard nothing.

Pasarian heard something, though. A new sound – the cries of the cadets as they choked and coughed and stumbled over one another in a desperate attempt to get out of the room. They were frantic and gasping for air. Their eyes were streaming with tears from the gas. Some of them already had minor blisters on their faces and hands.

Their guide ran toward a freight elevator and frantically pressed the button.

Nothing happened. That wasn't working either.

He pressed the button again and again, not knowing what else to do. His terror was less for his own life than for what he thought would happen to him if he survived and one of the Thorn boys did not.

The only person who wasn't panicking was Damien. The gas was having no effect upon him. He looked around at his friends as they began to collapse all around him, and for the first time, he felt the power of his being.

He also understood that he still had free will. He

could leave now and be the sole survivor, or he could help everyone else out and be the hero.

It was strangely beginning to make some sense to him now.

He decided to help. He suddenly loved the idea of being a hero. He quickly scanned the ceiling and saw a metal ladder bolted to one of the walls leading up to a hatchway which obviously let out onto the roof.

'Over here!' he cried, and ran to the ladder. Scaling it with lithe, hand-over-hand grace, he reached the portal at last, shoved it open, and let in a welcome rush of sunlight and fresh air.

The other cadets and the guide came stumbling and clambering along the catwalk, leaning on each other and helping one another along. They climbed their fumbling way up the ladder and out onto the roof, where they finally collapsed, spread-eagled, taking the air into their lungs with deep, heaving gulps.

Damien suddenly remembered Pasarian. He looked around to make sure everyone was accounted for, and then he turned and ducked back down inside, where he moved swiftly but cautiously along the highest catwalk. He sped down some metal stairs to the level below.

Nothing. No Pasarian,. Just the green noxious gas swirling and billowing and filling up the room. An alarm had started to sound, and red lights were flashing everywhere.

Damien ran around to the other side and took another set of stairs down to the next level.

And there he saw Pasarian. But Pasarian didn't see him.

Pasarian lay near the broken valve, crumpled up on the floor, one hand outstretched in a last, pathetic effort to twist it shut. His face, bloated and blistered, was practically unrecognizable.

He was very dead.

Damien turned his head away, repelled, and ran as fast as he could back toward the ladder.

Up on the roof, Damien reemerged to find the others still in panic, pain, and confusion as they rolled around on the tarpaper, choking, gasping, wheezing, tears streaming from their eyes.

He picked his way through the writhing bodies and moved toward Mark to check his condition.

And on the way, Damien realized he was beginning to like who he was after all.

CHAPTER NINE

Richard Thorn wanted to know what the hell had happened, and he wanted to know immediately.

He and Ann had left Lakeside the instant they heard the news; they flew into O'Hare, grabbed the first cab they could find, and rushed over to the Children's Hospital where the cadets had been taken after the accident.

Thorn stood, pale, unshaven, and shaking with rage, in the old army jacket he always wore for walks in the woods at Lake Geneva; he was talking to Buher on the wall phone in the corridor outside the boys' hospital room.

'They seem to be all right,' he said, 'but I haven't been able to talk to the doctor yet. I want a full report on what happened, and I want it on my desk in the morning!' He slammed down the phone and leaned heavily against the wall, exhausted.

Out of the corner of his eye, he noticed a tall, handsome black doctor walk into the boys' room. Thorn quickly followed him in, anxious to hear the results of the preliminary tests.

Ann was sitting on a chair between the two beds. Mark looked pale and weak, and held onto his mother's hand. Damien, however, appeared to be fine.

The doctor walked over to her and introduced himself as Dr Kane. Thorn was right behind him.

'They're going to be all right,' Kane said. 'We've tested every boy for lung damage. Not a sign of it.

143

They'll be nauseous for a while, but there's no permanent –'

'I want them *all* to have the best care possible,' Thorn interrupted.

Kane nodded his assurance. 'They will have,' he said, taking Thorn aside. 'May I see you in private for a moment?' he asked in a discreetly low voice.

'Of course,' said Thorn, and he followed the doctor back out into the hall.

From his bed, Damien watched them leave with great curiosity.

Out in the corridor, Kane waited until a passing orderly had moved out of earshot before he spoke. Thorn could tell from the look in Kane's eyes that something was troubling him deeply.

'We've made every possible test for blood and tissue damage,' he said, 'and every boy was affected to some degree – although, as I said, not seriously.' He paused. 'That is, every boy but your son Damien.'

A muscle in Thorn's face twitched involuntarily. 'What do you mean?' he asked. 'Is he –'

'No, no, Mr Thorn. It's not what you think.' Kane struggled to find the best way to explain it. 'You see,' he said, 'Damien wasn't affected . . . *at all*.'

Back in the hospital room, Damien questioned Ann. 'What do you think's going on?' His eyes were beginning to cloud over with dark and chilling fury.

Ann didn't seem to notice. She was concentrating on the door, awaiting Thorn's return. 'Oh, probably nothing,' she said. 'Doctors love secrets.'

When the two men came back into the room, Thorn looked very upset. 'The doctor wants Damien to stay here a couple of days,' he said, trying to sound casual. 'He'd like to do some more tests.'

144

Damien sat up. 'But I'm okay!' he protested. 'Why do I have to stay if –'

'Why do you want to do more tests?' Ann interrupted to ask Kane.

Thorn gave both of them a look that said 'Not in front of the boys.'

Damien cut in once more. 'I don't want to stay here!' Ann moved to take his in her arms.

Mark also rushed to his brother's aid. 'If he can't go, then I won't go!'

Ann looked across at the doctor and shrugged. 'Why can't we take him home now, and bring him back next week? It's been such a terrifying experience.'

'Would that be all right?' Thorn asked.

Kane didn't seem to like the idea, but he knew there was probably nothing he could do about it. 'Fine,' he said.

Ann smiled victoriously and gave Damien another hug. 'Okay, you guys,' she said to both of them, 'why don't you rest, and then we'll come by for you later and take you up to Lakeside, all right? The air will do you good.'

The boys nodded enthusiastically. They kissed their parents good-bye and watched them as they walked out with Dr Kane.

As they left, Damien studied Kane intently, as though trying to commit his face to memory.

Late that night, Dr Kane was still bent over his microscope, trying to understand the meaning of what he saw.

He was all alone in the hospital laboratory. He had skipped dinner, staying later than anyone else, and as he looked for perhaps the hundredth time at the thin sliver of blood on the glass plate under the microscope, he felt a faint shudder of revulsion, oddly coupled with the kind of thrill that comes only when a scientist has seen something he is sure no other man before him has ever seen.

He looked again at the book beside him, a thick, blue book with tiny print and meticulously detailed photographs, then back to the slide. There was no mistaking it.

Damien Thorn had the chromosome structure of a jackal.

It didn't make sense, it sounded like a bad joke, and yet here was seemingly irrefutable proof with which Kane's logical mind was forced to cope.

Somehow he didn't want to deal with it alone. On the chance that a respected friend and colleague of his was still in his office at this hour, Kane picked up the phone and dialed an extension number he knew by heart.

Kane was about to hang up after about seven rings, when a voice suddenly crackled across the line. 'Yes?'

'Ben!' cried Kane. 'Thank God you're still in! May I come down and see you for a second?'

'Well,' came the crackling voice, 'I was just on my way out.'

'Please,' said Kane. 'It's urgent!'

'All right then,' his colleague replied, 'come on down.'

'Thanks, Ben. I'll see you in a minute.' Kane hung up the phone, put the slide carefully into a container, tucked the book under one arm, and headed for the elevator.

At Lakeside, almost everyone was sound asleep. Only Damien was not lost in slumber. His body was absolutely rigid, and his eyes, though open and focused, were looking at nothing in the room. They seemed to be looking at something *somewhere* else, and he was having to concentrate on it very hard. So hard, in fact, that sweat broke out on his forehead and his body began to tremble.

Dr Kane stepped into the elevator and pressed the button to go down to the sixteenth floor. The doors glided shut and the elevator began to move.

But rather than down, the elevator went *up*.

Kane checked the overhead floor indicator: 21 . . . 22 . . . 23 . . . He pressed 16 again. The elevator stopped and its doors opened.

But no one was there. Kane pushed 16 a third time.

The doors shut, and the elevator finally began to descend: 19 . . . 18 . . . 17 . . .

It went right past the sixteenth floor and kept on going, picking up speed as it went.

Kane was terrified and confused. He threw down the book and the slide and tried pushing every button on the panel. They all lit up and started flashing. The elevator was gaining momentum and beginning to shake violently.

10 . . . 9 . . . . 8 . . .

'My God!' Kane screamed, pounding on the panel, pushing every button, flipping every switch.

5 . . . 4 . . . 3 . . .

The elevator suddenly lurched to a stop, throwing Kane to the floor. In the dead silence that followed, Kane lay very still, afraid to move, afraid even to breathe.

Slowly, carefully, he rolled over and sat up. He couldn't believe it. He felt himself all over, checking for broken bones, anything, but he was seemingly all right – shaken, but not hurt. He noticed that the slide had shattered, but he didn't care. He was so glad to be alive.

High up above him, in the elevator shaft, a single cable had snapped from the pressure of the elevator's sudden stop, and now was lashing down the shaft like a giant, lethal whip.

It was then that Kane heard the noise; a high, piercing, metallic whine. He looked around but could not tell where the noise was coming from. Finally he looked up — just in time to see the cable rip viciously through the roof of the elevator and slice down through the floor, cutting him in half in the process.

Damien's body finally relaxed; his eyes closed, and he slept with a peace he had not known since the strange stirrings had begun inside him on the sixth day of June.

CHAPTER TEN

Richard and Ann lay in bed, reading the morning papers brought up' to them along with breakfast. Richard always read *The Wall Street Journal* first, while Ann preferred *The Chicago Tribune*.

This morning, when Ann opened the paper, she gasped. 'Richard! Look!' she said, passing the newspaper across to him.

It was a gruesome photograph of the late Dr Kane, with an accompanying story on the elevator accident the night before, with a short account of the gas leak accident at Thorn Industries.

Thorn was momentarily more concerned about how the story of the accident at the plant was handled than the account of the doctor's death.

'We were with him just yesterday,' Ann said, twisting a strand of hair between her fingers. 'Doesn't that make you feel weird?'

'Hmmmmm . . .'

Ann took a sip of coffee and looked over at Richard. 'What kind of tests did Dr Kane want to make, anyway?'

'I'm not sure,' Richard said. 'I don't think *he* even –' he broke off suddenly. 'Where are the boys?' he asked.

'Asleep, I suppose. Why?'

Richard put the papers down and shifted around to look at Ann. 'I just don't want them to hear about this.'

'Why?' Ann was concerned. 'What did the doctor tell you?'

'It seems that Damien was unaffected by the gas.'

'What's so bad about that? We should all be grateful . . .'

'It certainly bothered the doctor,' Richard said. 'He said he went over Damien's tests half a dozen times.'

'And . . . ?'

'I don't know,' said Richard. 'It had something to do with his chromosomes being different.'

'Different?' said Ann. 'That's absurd!'

'That's what I said, too,' Richard replied, 'but Dr Kane seemed awfully concerned about it.

Ann sat quietly for a moment, then said, 'What do you want to do about it?'

'Nothing, if you want to know the truth.' Richard reached for the *Journal* again. 'I just don't buy that sort of genetic nonsense. Damien's perfectly fine.'

Why Damien awoke that morning with a terrible migraine headache was a mystery to everyone, especially to Damien.

Dr Charles Warren had just returned from Acre, where he had supervised the painstaking work of crating and shipping the last few artifacts of the Belvoir dig which were going to be used in the Thorn Museum exhibit.

By some fluke, he had missed seeing Yigael's Wall. The priceless artifact had already been packed and shipped before he had arrived. He was quite disappointed about this; ever since his late friend, journalist Joan Hart, had made such a spectacle of herself over the wall, he had been curious indeed to see it. And now he would have to wait until it arrived in Chicago, unless he went to New York when the boat came in.

He was glad to be back in the States, and especially glad to be back in his office. He thought he had the best workroom in the entire museum. Located on the basement level, adjacent to the boiler room, it provided all the quiet and privacy he needed in his work, particularly at times like tonight, when the museum was closed and everyone else had already gone home.

His quarters were well supplied with all the latest equipment necessary for the maintenance and restoration of ancient artifacts: special air conditioners, special infrared and ultraviolet lights, portable heaters equipped with their own individual thermostats, bottled chemicals, special brushes and palette knives. With this odd combination of ancient instruments and the latest technology, Warren was able to make a centuries-old fresco look as good as new without doing damage to the artist's original conception, and without using any materials other than those available to the artist at the time.

At the moment, Warren was going through some of the things that had been shipped in one of the batches of goods from Acre. He pushed aside some bronze knives and shards of pottery, and moved out an ancient-looking leather box. This was one of the items he had personally carried back on the plane, and suspecting its importance, he had waited until the right moment to examine it thoroughly, and in private.

He undid all the leather straps carefully and pulled them free. Then he opened the box, looked in, and sniffed. Although he could tell that it wasn't truly ancient, it didn't seem new either.

He reached into the box gingerly and pulled out some tightly wrapped parchment scrolls. These, he set aside. He reached in again. This time, he produced a small crucifix, with a terribly agonized Christ carved upon it. Warren stared at the object. He set it to one side and plunged his hand into the box yet again. Out came, of all things, a modern manila envelope! Although he was intrigued, he put that too aside for the time being.

There was one more object in the leather box.

Warren reached in for the fourth and final time, and pulled out a rather heavy bundle wrapped in an old and weather-worn fabric: as he drew it out, something clinked. Warren carefully unwrapped the cloth, revealing seven thin stilettos, very sharp, but obviously very old. They were ivory-handled, each handle carved into the form of Christ on the cross.

By this time, Warren's curiosity was overwhelming. He picked up the manila envelope and slit it open, sliding out a fairly thick pile of papers. Fascinating, he thought, as he examined it. The handwriting looks like Carl Bugenhagen's.

And then he sat down to read.

With the boys home during mid-term, the Thorns were having a rare family evening, watching an especially exciting Western in their den.

On the screen, a tall man walked down the only street of a dusty cattle town, hands loosely at his sides, inches from his pearl-handled guns.

He didn't see the blunt snout of the Winchester protruding from the third-floor window of the hotel, or the fluttering of the sash at the second-floor window of the supposedly empty feed store across the street.

Then the Winchester barked, and the man flopped over, then multiplied, went fuzzy, and skidded off the screen and onto the wall.

'Shoot the projectionist!' shouted Damien.

Mark stuck his head out of the small aperture in the wall behind Damien and shouted back, 'Drop dead!' Then he turned back earnestly to try to fix the projector.

Ordinarily, the butler ran the projection machine when the Thorns watched movies at home, but Mark had pleaded to be taught how to run it, and his father had agreed. Here he was on his first time out, with just his father and mother and Damien watching, and he had screwed up the movie right at the best part.

But luckily he soon got it going again, to the accompaniment of Damien's falsely compassionate advice, just in time for the hero to get up off his back and make magnificent double play – his right-hand gun dropped the man with the Winchester three floors to the street, while his left sent the man behind the fluttering shade bouncing onto the porch roof of the feed store, and from there into a horse trough. Then the hero leaped onto his horse from behind and rode off into the sunset, to the mighty applause of all.

'Well! A happy ending for a change!' Ann said, as Damien switched on the lights.

'I give it a six,' Damien said.

Ann smiled and shook her head. 'You're too young to be so cynical.' She stood up and stretched. 'Who wants a corned beef sandwich?'

'One!' Richard raised his hand.

'Two!' added Damien.

'I know Mark will want one,' Ann said, and she left to go to the kitchen to prepare them.

In the projection booth, Mark was carefully rewinding the film, trying not to get it caught again. In the den, Damien was folding up the screen to put it away, while Richard set up the backgammon board.

When the doorbell rang, interrupting them, Richard and Damien shared a 'Who could that be?' look. Damien shrugged; 'I'll get it,' he said, and headed for the front door.

Charles Warren stood there, cold and covered with snow. In his hands he held Bugenhagen's manila envelope. He was trembling, and not entirely from the cold. He had just read something that scared him – literally almost to death.

Warren nearly fainted when the front door opened and he saw Damien before him. He tried to smile, but Damien sensed something immediately and was instantly on guard.

'Hello, Dr Warren,' he said tersely.

'Well, hello, Damien.' Warren was obviously trying to keep his voice under control. 'Would you tell your father I'd like to see him, please?'

'Is he expecting you?' Damien was cool, formal, not giving an inch.

'Just tell him I'm here, please,' Warren said, a hint of steel coming into his voice.

Damien hesitated for an instant, then said, 'Come in.'

Warren stepped into the hallway, and Damien shut the door behind him. 'I'll tell him you're here,' he said, and he walked back to the den. Warren shook the snow off his jacket, and waited, trying to think of what he was going to say.

'It's Dr Warren,' Damien told his father. 'He wants to see you.'

'Charles?' said Richard, both pleased and surprised. 'Great! Send him in!'

But Warren, unable to wait any longer, had already entered the room behind Damien.

'Ask your mother to make another sandwich for Dr Warren,' Richard said to Damien, who left the room without another word, shutting the door firmly behind him.

Once alone in the hallway, Damien's expression became cold, furious. He didn't need anyone to tell him what Warren was doing here, or why he was looking at him like that. Nor was there anything he could do about it – at the moment. He went off to the kitchen to order the extra sandwich as he had been told to do.

Warren had taken a seat and was watching with some apprehension as Richard poured out two brandies. Warren didn't quite know where to begin.

Thorn had forgotten about Mark, who was still rewinding the last reel of the Western up in the booth,

154

where it was impossible for him not to hear every word of Dr Warren's conversation with his father.

Warren accepted the brandy from Thorn and took such a large gulp that his host looked at him in surprise. Taking courage from the alcohol, he decided to plunge right in. 'Richard,' he said, looking down at the floor, 'I have to ask you something very personal.'

'We're friends, Charles,' Richard said assuringly. 'Go ahead.'

Warren took a deep breath and then blurted, 'Can you tell me what actually happened to your brother in London?'

Richard Thorn's voice and attitude suddenly changed and took on the cold stiffness that all his friends and associates had come to recognize as a signal that someone was out of line. 'Why do you ask?' he managed to say.

'I've just opened a box I found at Acre. It belonged to Bugenhagen, contained his most personal effects. They found it near his body.'

'So?' Thorn said, in a tone that implied he was losing his patience.

Warren took another long gulp of brandy. 'Did you know it was Bugenhagen who gave your brother the daggers to kill Damien?'

Thorn whirled around. 'What the hell are you talking about?'

In the projection booth behind them, Mark moved to the aperture and listened to the startling conversation.

'Seven years ago,' Warren went on, 'Bugenhagen wrote you a letter –'

'A letter? To me?' Thorn began to pace. 'I never got any letter.'

'He never sent it,' Warren said. 'It was still in the box . . .'

'You've read it?' Thorn asked accusingly.

Warren was pleading now. 'Richard,' he said, 'you

know me. You know I'm a rational man. But what I'm about to tell you won't sound rational at all.'

'Just tell me, Warren, for God's sake!'

'Bugenhagen claims that Damien . . .' Warren swallowed hard, 'that Damien . . . is an instrument of the Devil. Anti-Christ!'

Thorn stared at Warren as if he had gone mad.

In the projection booth, Mark caught his breath.

Warren plunged on: 'He isn't human, Richard. I know it sounds crazy, but Bugenhagen claims he was born of a jackal!'

Thorn started to laugh. 'You bothered to *tell* me this?' He shook his head and started to walk away.

Warren finished off his brandy and set the glass down. 'Your brother found out,' he said, following Thorn. 'He went to Bugenhagen, desperate for advice. Bugenhagen told him how to kill the boy.'

Thorn banged his own drink down on the table and turned around to face Warren. 'My brother was ill,' he said icily. 'Mentally ill. His wife's death –'

'– was caused by Damien!' Warren broke in. 'And all the other deaths . . . five inexplicable deaths. It's seemingly part of prophesies made in the Book of Revelation.' Warren knew he was treading on dangerous ground, but he had to go on, no matter how angry Thorn was. 'Bugenhagen –'

'Who was obviously insane,' Thorn interrupted.

Warren shook his head in frustration and fear. 'I know it all *sounds* insane . . .' he admitted.

'But you believe it,' Thorn said.

Warren pulled Bugenhagen's letter out of his pocket and tossed it on the table. 'Here's the letter,' he said. 'Read it yourself.'

'No.'

'If Bugenhagen is right,' Warren insisted, 'we're all in danger. You, Ann, Mark – all of us. Remember what happened to Joan Hart – she *knew*.'

156

Thorn was adamant. 'I have no intention of reading the ravings of a senile old man,' he said.

'Richard,' Warren begged, 'I knew Bugenhagen. He wasn't senile. Haven't you had any suspicions? Hasn't anything strange –'

'No!' Thorn shouted.

Warren was afraid Thorn was going to hit him, but he persisted. 'Nothing the boy has said or done?' he said. 'Nothing that's happened?'

'I want you out of my house, Charles . . .'

'There have been deaths among us, too.'

'*Get out*!' Thorn said, shaking with rage.

But Warren couldn't stop. 'The signs are too clear, Richard,' he said. 'The coincidences are too strong to be ignored. Read in the Bible – the Book of Revelation – it's all there! We have to follow this thing through to the end!'

'What end?' Thorn asked, amazed that he was even tolerating this discussion.

'Yigael's Wall,' said Warren, breathing heavily by now. 'Bugenhagen says in his letter that the Wall was the final thing that convinced him. It's on its way to New York. It'll be there any day now.'

'You've been grubbing around in the past too long,' said Thorn. 'You've become a religious maniac like your friend Joan Hart. I won't have any part of it. *You* go look at it!'

Warren looked at him for a long moment. He hadn't expected it to be easy, but neither had he thought it would end this way. He knew his relationship with Thorn might soon be over, but he had no choice but to go on. 'I will,' he said softly, and left, closing the door gently behind him.

Thorn sat down in his chair, stunned. Some of what Warren had said was possibly true, to be sure, and it was disconcerting that he'd gotten the information at all; but as for the rest of it . . .

Thorn shook his head. He felt he had just lost a very good friend, and he could not even say why.

In the projection booth, Mark was shaking like a leaf. He reached for the aperture door and pulled it closed as quickly and as quietly as possible.

Damien was helping Ann make sandwiches in the kitchen. They both heard the front door slam, and the sound of Warren starting up his car, the tires squealing on the driveway.

They looked at one another, then at the extra sandwich they had just made.

'Oh, well,' said Damien brightly, 'I guess I'll just have to eat two!'

CHAPTER ELEVEN

Damien's sleep was as untroubled as a thirteen-year-old boy's should be.

Ann slept peacefully, too.

But Richard Thorn did not, and neither did Mark.

It was dawn at the house on the lake, and both Thorn and his son were awake.

Thorn, tired and drawn, was still in his clothes from the night before. He sat at the desk in his study, his head in his hands as he tried desperately to think what to do. Spread out before him was the long-delayed letter Bugenhagen had written him, which he had now read and reread several times over. The implications in the letter were too enormous, too unbelievable, for him to be able to absorb it all at once. He needed much more time to think.

He gathered up the pages and locked them away in his desk. Then he stood up and stretched. He walked over to the window. The sun was just beginning to spill light across the distant snow-covered hills. It cannot be true, he said to himself. There is no such thing as the Devil, except as he exists in men's minds.

Then he turned and went upstairs, to try to get at least a couple hours' sleep.

Unknown to Thorn, Mark, too, had been up all night. He had pretended to go to sleep, and when the house was quiet and still, he had slipped out of bed and stolen down into the library. There he had taken the big family Bible off the shelf and had begun to read the Book of Revelation.

And now, as the light of dawn crept in through the library window, Mark looked up from the pages of the book and started to cry, both from weariness at having been up all night and from the terrifying knowledge he had so recently gained.

For Mark now believed totally that Damien was indeed the son of the Devil.

He thought about Damien's odd behaviour in the past few months, and his performance in history class that bewildering day not long ago. He thought about his prowess on the athletic field and the way he apparently could do no wrong.

He also remembered how everyone but Damien had been affected by the gas that day at the plant. He thought of Pasarian, and Atherton, and Aunt Marion, and all the other people who were dying, suddenly and inexplicably, around them.

And finally he thought of his cousin whom he loved, whom he practically worshipped. Was it possible that other people – terrible, loathesome people – worshipped his cousin too, but in a much different way?

Mark got up and put the Bible back where he had found it. Then he tiptoed softly into the front hall, pulled his heavy winter overcoat off the rack, and put it on, slipping quietly out the front door. He wanted to get away for a while, to think about what to do . . .

'Damien is what?' asked Ann, turning around from the stove where she was fixing scrambled eggs. 'You can't *believe* that, Richard –'

'I didn't say I believed it, Ann,' said Richard, standing in the doorway to the kitchen with Bugenhagen's letter in his hands. 'I'm only telling you what Charles said, and what's written in this letter.'

'But you're thinking of going to New York, for Christ's sake!' Ann threw down the spatula and went over to the cupboard to get some dishes. She couldn't

160

believe she was having this conversation. 'Doesn't that mean –'

'No!' Richard shouted. He was so tired from having stayed up the night before that he didn't have the energy to be reasonable. 'It's disgusting nonsense, and of *course* I don't believe it. But Robert *was* shot in a church trying to stab Damien, and –'

'Warren's gotten to you, hasn't he?' Ann went over to the table and put the dishes down. 'He's planted his craziness in you.' She walked over to him, took Bugenhagen's letter from his hands and laid it on the counter, and then took both his hands in her own. 'Well, I'm not going to let you be poisoned by it,' she said firmly. 'You're tired and you're not thinking straight. You're not going anywhere. You're going to forget you ever spoke to –'

'Ann –'

'No. It's over. You heard a stupid, filthy story and it's *over*.' Suddenly she burst into tears. 'Oh, Richard!' she cried, 'what's happening to us? Have we all gone mad?'

Richard took her in his arms and held her close. 'Don't cry,' he said compassionately. 'You're right. I'm tired and overworked. I'm sorry, so sorry . . .'

'Oh God, please,' Ann murmured, burying her face in his shoulder.

'Shh . . . it's all right. I'm not going anywhere.'

'And Damien – you're not to look at him any differently, or treat him any –'

'No, no, of course not.'

'Promise me.'

'I promise.'

As Richard stood there holding onto his wife, rocking her gently in his arms and wondering how he could have gotten so carried away, he looked out the kitchen window and saw Damien walking across the back lawn, heading into the woods.

161

The sight triggered alarm in him.

'Where's Mark?' he asked, trying to sound casual.

'I guess he went out early,' Ann replied, drawing back from Richard and wiping her eyes. 'I noticed his overcoat was missing from the rack when I went to get the paper this morning.'

'Why don't we go for a walk, too?' Richard suggested.

'But the eggs –' They had started to burn, and she rush to the stove to rescue them.

'I could really use some air.'

Ann stared at her husband. Something was going on in their household, in their family, that she did not entirely understand. When she had married Thorn, she knew it was not going to be easy, but she had loved him so much that she felt she could overcome and withstand any and all crises. Now she wasn't so sure.

She shrugged and put the pan with the eggs into the sink. 'Okay,' she said lightly. 'A walk it is.'

Mark sat at the base of a tree far away from the house. He looked pale and quite worried. His eyes were sick with fear, and held a look much older than a boy his age should ever have. His arms were wrapped tightly around his knees, more from fear than from the cold, for he had never been so afraid in all his life.

And he didn't know to whom he could turn for comfort. He had always gone to Damien before with his troubles, but he couldn't do so now. He would have to handle this one alone.

Then Mark heard footsteps; a voice called out, 'Mark? Hey, Mark!'

It was Damien of course. Always Damien.

Mark got to his feet very quickly and very quietly, and moved deeper into the woods.

Damien was following his tracks.

Mark started to run.

'Hey, *Mark*!'

Mark ran on, but he knew he could not run too far. He hadn't slept the night before; he was exhausted and terribly frightened. He finally came to a very large, thick-trunked tree, and he hid there behind it, panting for breath.

A few minutes passed, and he heard Damien's voice again, very close now. Just on the other side of the tree. 'I know you're there,' Damien said.

Mark trembled. 'Leave me alone,' he said sounding weak even to himself.

Damien made a wide circle around the trunk coming to a stop some six feet in front of Mark. 'Why are you running away from me?' He actually sounded distressed.

There was a long pause. Finally Mark said in a hushed voice, 'I know . . . who you are.'

Damien smiled. 'You do?'

Mark nodded. 'Dr Warren knows,' he said carefully. 'I heard him talking to Dad.'

Damien's face clouded over slightly. 'What did he say?' It was more a command than a question.

'He said' – Mark struggled to find the words – 'he said that the Devil could create his image on earth.'

'Go on.'

Mark looked away. A tear rolled down his cheek.

'Say it, Mark,' said Damien very quietly.

Mark swallowed hard. 'He said . . . you're a son of the Devil.'

In another part of the woods, Ann and Richard strolled together in silence. From a distance one would have thought that they were two lovers out on an early morning walk, after having spent the night wrapped in each other's arms.

But this man walking with his lady had eyes that were bloodshot from worried exhaustion, and his mind was obviously racing. He was clearly on the lookout for something that he fervently hoped he would not find . . .

Damien stared hard at Mark. 'Keep on going,' he said.

And finally it all came tumbling out. 'I saw what you did to Teddy in the hall that day,' Mark shouted, 'and I saw what happened in the classroom; and I saw what happened to Atherton and Pasarian! Your father tried to kill you!' he cried. 'They say he was crazy, but it was because he *knew*!' Mark fell to his knees, shaking.

Damien was becoming perturbed. He didn't want to hurt Mark.

'Mark –' he began.

'Nooooo . . .' wailed Mark.

'You're my brother. I love you –'

'Don't call me your brother!' Mark cried. 'The Anti-Christ has no brother!'

Damien grabbed Mark by the shoulders. 'Listen to me!' he shouted.

Mark shook his head. 'Admit it,' he blurted out, 'you killed your own mother!'

That did it. That snapped the bond. 'She was *not* my mother!' bellowed Damien. 'My mother –'

'– was a *jackal*.'

'Yes!' cried Damien proudly, his voice echoing through the woods. He was in full command of his power now. His eyes burned brightly, and his face took on a glow that was clearly not human. 'I was born in the image of the greatest power in the world,' he said, his voice growing in intensity. 'The Nail!' he cried. 'The Desolate One! Desolate because his greatness was taken from him and he was cast down. But he has *risen in me*! He is looking through *my* eyes and he is wearing *my* body!'

Mark looked around desperately. He was beyond fear; he felt listless, incapable of movement. It was like a

164

horrible dream, an endless nightmare, and he could not escape it.

'Come with me,' said Damien. 'I can take you with me.'

Mark looked up. He stopped trembling and stared at his cousin for a long time, then finally, slowly shaking his head, he said, 'No.'

Damien pleaded. 'Don't make me beg you!'

Mark remained firm. 'No.'

And then as if his denial had given him newfound strength, Mark vaulted from the ground and started to run as fast as his tired limbs could move.

'Mark!' Damien shouted after him.

But Mark kept on running. 'Get away from me!' he yelled back.

'MARK!' Damien shouted in a voice that Mark had heard only once before, in the hallway outside of Neff's office when Damien had called out to Teddy. '*Look at me!*' he commanded.

Mark stopped in his tracks. He found himself unable to move. 'Please get away,' he begged.

But Damien's voice held him there. 'I'll ask you once more,' he said calmly, in full control now. 'Please. Come with me. Be mine!'

Mark turned around slowly until he faced his cousin directly. 'No,' he said, with a sudden calm even stronger than Damien's. 'You can't escape your destiny, Damien. And I can't escape mine.' Some other force was speaking through him. 'You must do what you have to do.' And he stood there, suspended, waiting.

A rage entered Damien, a rage borne of rejection, and as the fire blazed even more brightly in his eyes, he stood up tall, to a height that now seemed suddenly immense. Tears welled up in his eyes, and he looked up to the sky and began to tremble . . .

Richard and Ann had found the boys' footprints in the

snow and were following them. Ann seemed very calm as she walked at her husband's side, leaning against him from time to time. But Richard kept glancing up, as if sensing something foreboding in the air.

Suddenly Mark heard the sound, the same sound Teddy had heard in the hallway that day outside Sergeant Neff's office.

A clattering, like thin metal rulers being clapped together.

The sound of raven's wings.

Mark thrust out his arms to protect his head against the invisible thing that was attacking him. He screamed, he cried, he tried to get away, but the dreadful beak and claws of the invisible bird tore at his head until blood began to drip from his nostrils, from his eyes, even from his ears. He fell to his knees in pain and howled, and all he could see through the blood that coursed across his eyes was the evil sight of Damien: erect, relentless, at his full height, haloed by the rising sun behind him – implacable and impossible to fight against.

And then the bird's beak seemed to cleave Mark's skull and penetrate his brain. The boy fell forward into the snow, his face a ghostly white, his eyes rolled back into his head.

The whirring sound ceased. Damien looked down and let out a cry, a sweet and desolate wail, as he saw the dead body of Mark lying in the snow, which was slowly turning red from the flow of blood. He ran over to Mark, knelt down and scooped up the frail and lifeless body in his arms, and tried to restore him to life.

Damien's wail of agony carried back to Ann and Richard. When they arrived, they found Damien bending over the lifeless body of his cousin, moaning, 'Mark, oh Mark . . .'

At the sound of Ann's scream, Damien looked up and

166

jumped back. 'We were just walking –' he said, '– and he fell! He just –'

'Get back to the house,' Richard yelled. He ran over to Ann, who was kneeling beside the lifeless body of Mark.

Damien started to protest. 'I didn't do anything.'

'Get back to the house, *damn you*!' Richard was trembling with rage.

Damien turned and started to run in the direction of the house, tears beginning to stream down his face. 'He fell!' he shouted over his shoulder. 'I didn't do anything!' But he kept on running.

Richard turned away from the retreating figure and bent over his wife. Taking her by the shoulders, he lifted her gently from the ground.

When he saw she could stand on her own, he bent down again and picked up the body of his dead son.

Then he stood up and turned to face Ann. There was a look of accusation in his eyes.

Ann shook her head and stammered, 'It wasn't Damien. He didn't –'

She never finished the sentence. Richard turned from his wife and walked away, pressing his face against the bloody face of his lifeless son.

CHAPTER TWELVE

The Thorn family cemetery plot was on the North Shore, not far from the estate. Reginald Thorn was buried there beside his wife; Richard's first wife, Mary, was there too, and Aunt Marion was not far off in a place by herself.

They buried Mark next to his mother.

And one day, Richard Thorn thought, as he stared blankly through the dismal winter drizzle at the gathering around the small gravesite, I will be here, too.

Both Ann and Richard wore black. Damien, standing next to Ann, was dressed simply and appropriately in his navy blue uniform with a black armband around his left arm.

Paul Buher was there, representing Thorn Industries. And Sergeant Neff had arrived with a small honor guard from the Academy. As the coffin was lowered into the grave, the honor guard stood at attention and a lone cadet stepped forward with his bugle and began to play 'Taps.'

As the first notes sounded, Ann started to cry. Thorn was reminded, oddly, of an old cowboy song he and his brother, Robert, used to sing around the bonfire when they camped out with their Academy buddies as kids: 'There's an empty bed in the bunkhouse tonight . . .' The memory brought tears to his eyes, and he wept for the first time since his son had died.

As the priest began the funeral prayer, Richard looked away. He didn't want to hear what the man had to say; there was no way the priest could possibly capture the specific essence of his son Mark. Priests and ministers were forced to speak in clichés, but the last thing Richard needed to hear at this moment was some platitude about his only son.

His glance fell on Damien and what he saw held his attention. The boy was looking over at Neff, who in turn was gazing at Buher, who was concentrated on Damien. A neat little triangle.

But before Thorn had time to think about that, he felt a tugging at his sleeve; he turned to find Ann looking at him with a tear-stained face, pleading with her eyes for him to pay attention, to offer some respect to the ceremony.

Richard patted her hand and then faced the grave again, struggling to listen to the words of the priest, searching for some meaning in what he was chanting. But he was soon back to sorting out his own mixed feelings about the events of the past few days.

He kept going back to the conversation he had had in Dr Fiedler's office, after the autopsy had been performed.

'How could it have happened?' he had asked the doctor. 'You've seen him ever since he was born. Shouldn't there have been some sign?'

The doctor had shaken his head sadly. 'I've seen it happen before, I'm afraid,' he had said. 'A perfectly normal boy – or man – healthy in all respects it seems; but there it is, waiting in his brain for some undue strain – a thin artery wall. The wall goes –' He had spread his hands wide in a gesture of compassion and inevitability.

At that point, Ann had interjected, 'Then it was there from the time he was born?'

Dr Fiedler had nodded. 'More than likely,' he had said gently. 'I'm sorry. I'm very sorry.'

But not as sorry as I am, Richard had thought.

The funeral was over now and the group of mourners moved away from the grave. It had begun to rain heavily, so everyone hurried through their condolences and then rushed off to get into the waiting cars.

Richard lingered until everyone had been acknowledged with a tight smile or touch of hands, and then ducked into his limousine and took his place next to Ann and Damien. He gave the signal to Murray, and the car pulled slowly away.

Very late at night the following week, a phone call came to the Thorn residence from New York. The call was from a priest; he asked Richard to come right away, that Dr Charles Warren was in very bad shape, and that he had been asking repeatedly for Richard Thorn.

In a matter of minutes, Richard threw some things into a suitcase. Ann tried to convince him to stay at least until the morning, but he wouldn't hear of it. He had to go at once.

'I don't *want* to go,' he shouted at Ann, 'I *have* to!'

Ann sat up in bed and reached for a cigarette. Her hands were shaking. 'Why can't you call back and talk to Charles over the phone?' she asked. 'Why do you have to go all the way to New York? It isn't as though Charles Warren has been such a good friend to this family recently.'

'They said he's in grave trouble and he needs me,' interrupted Thorn, looking around the room to see if he had forgotten anything.

'We need you, too,' said Ann quietly.

Richard turned and looked at her. 'I'll be back as soon as possible.' He leaned down and kissed her on the cheek, then moved toward the door.

'What will I tell Damien in the morning?' she asked.

Richard hesitated in the doorway. He hadn't thought of that. 'Tell him,' he said, thinking fast, 'tell him I had to go help Charles with urgent customs problems in

170

New York. Tell him anything. Just don't tell him the truth!' And he hurried from the room, closing the door softly behind him.

And as he tiptoed down the stairs to join the waiting Murray who stood bleary-eyed by the idling limousine, Thorn failed to notice the door to Damien's bedroom opening slightly and the narrowing, yellow cat-like eyes that penetrated the darkness behind him.

As soon as Richard had settled in his seat on the plane, and the jet had taken off from Meigs airport, he switched on the overhead light and pulled Bugenhagen's letter out of his carry-on suitcase. There was so much he had to think about, so much to absorb, and he was beginning to feel that there wasn't much time. He checked his watch. Four thirty A.M. He would be in New York by seven thirty or eight at the latest, their time. Just as the city was waking up.

Thorn looked back at the pages in front of him and began to read for the fourth or fifth time:

> And he had power to give life unto the image of the beast should both speak, and cause that as many as would not worship the image of the beast should be killed.

Thorn shuddered. There had been so many deaths in the past few months – too many to be purely coincidential. The pieces were at last beginning to fall into place.

First, there had been Aunt Marion. Her voice echoed in his memory. *Damien's a terrible influence, can't you see it*? she had said. *Do you want to ruin Mark, destroy him*?

And then that reporter, Joan Hart. A horrible horrible death she had apparently suffered, from the brief newspaper account. And so needlessly. *You're in grave danger*! she had warned. *Put your faith in Christ*!

And Atherton. Another unbelievably gruesome death. But where did he fit in? Thorn wasn't sure. Pasarian's death made no sense either.

Thorn read on:

> And through his policy also shall he cause craft to prosper in his hand, and he shall magnify himself in his heart, and by peace shall destroy many . . .

Thorn thought of his company, one of the largest multinational corporations in the world, and how Damien would someday inherit it. And more things began to make sense. Atherton had resisted Buher's plan to move into the production and distribution of food, and Atherton had died. Buher became president, and his plan was being put into effect. But not without troubles. Pasarian found out about those troubles, and Pasarian had died.

Someday, if things went according to plan, Damien would inherit an industry that controlled the feeding of the world population.

Thorn remembered the funeral that afternoon and the odd triangular connection between Damien and Buher and Neff. But where did Neff fit in? Thorn turned back to the Bugenhagen's notes to try to find a clue:

> And all the world wondered after the beast. And they worshipped the dragon which gave power to the beast. And they worshipped the beast, saying, 'Who is like unto the beast? Who is able to make war with Him?'

The dragon.
Perhaps Neff was the dragon, a military strategist, there to teach and to train . . .

And it was given unto him to make war with the saints, *and to overcome them*: and power was given him over all kindreds and tongues, and notions . . . And he shall also stand up against the Prince of Princes . . .

Thorn couldn't read anymore. His eyes were beginning to ache and his thoughts were becoming fuzzy. He simply wasn't capable of clear thinking any longer. He needed some rest, just a few hours' sleep.

He was haunted by what Warren had said the night he showed them the slides from the dig: *There is a great deal of evidence that the end of the world is near.* Ann had laughed, but Warren had gone on to mention some of the biblical prophecies that were only now beginning to come true – all at once. Floods, famine, darkness, wars . . .

Thorn thought about some of the alarming events that had happened in the world recently. The situation in the Middle East could still erupt into an all-out war that would probably involve the rest of the world, precipitating what would later be known as World War III, if anyone lived to call it that.

Nuclear proliferation had accelerated at a terrifying rate. Almost every single nation in the world, industrial or not, had their hands on some kind of nuclear bomb. All that was needed was one mad terrorist in some remote section of the world to set off a bomb, for the most ridiculous and narrow-minded of reasons – and an inevitable and irreversible chain reaction would be triggered, each nation trying to bomb the others into oblivion before it was bombed.

New York wasn't the only city to suffer a blackout that year. London, Paris, Moscow, and Tokyo all underwent mysterious power failures. Sabotage was suspected in every case, but no evidence to support that suspicion was ever found. And in every case, the looting and the pillage and the rape and the killing that went on was worse than anyone had ever believed imaginable. And no city was better or worse than another. They were all equally horrifying.

Human beings seemed to be turning into machines, reacting without sensitivity, without compassion. They were all on a treadmill, moving too fast and too furiously to think, subjected to so many disappointments and such frequent and random violence that they were all turning inward, isolating themselves from those around them and from the rest of the world at large.

And the weather patterns had become odd and inexplicable. There was snow where there had never been snow before, droughts where there had always been rain, floods in terrain that had always been bone-dry. Hurricanes, tornadoes, and earthquakes seemed to be ravaging the earth more frequently than ever before. It was hard to tell whether there were really more disasters, or whether the world was just made more aware of them through increased communication technology. But the effect was the same. It *seemed* like more.

Thorn could not concentrate any longer. His eyelids fluttered with exhaustion and soon closed completely, and he fell into a shallow and still troubled sleep.

CHAPTER THIRTEEN

It was light when the smallest of the Thorn Industries jets taxied onto a distant runway at La Guardia airport. Inside the jet, Thorn stretched and yawned and checked his watch. Seven forty-five A.M.

He suddenly felt like a fool. He couldn't believe he had flown a thousand miles because of a phone call in the middle of the night from some strange sounding priest who said that Warren needed him. The last time he had seen Warren, they had bitterly quarrelled and Warren had left in a huff. Thorn had been sure they would never be civil to one another again.

But the information that Warren had tried to share with him that night, and which Thorn had then so adamantly refused to accept, had become a serious possibility for him. Now he, too, felt utterly compelled to see things through to the end.

He was sure that Warren had seen the Wall, that this was what he meant that Thorn must see for himself.

It troubled him that a priest had made the call rather than Warren himself. Perhaps it was some arcane form of protection at which Warren was grasping. Thorn had no way of knowing.

He walked through the terminal and hailed a cab outside, giving the directions received the night before from the priest. The cab driver looked askance at Thorn, then shrugged and pulled the flag down on his meter, and they drove off quickly.

During the ride, Thorn thought about a heated political discussion he had had once with his brother,

Robert, who had won his argument with a quote from Lenin. It was typical of Robert that he could incorporate all the ranges of political thought and rhetoric, and make some wonderful sense out of it all for his own use in a debate. The quotation that now came to Richard's mind was the question Lenin had forced himself to ask of every action: Who does this benefit?

Thorn applied that question now to everything he had gone over the night before. He was sure he had been overly emotional, overly anxious to have all the pieces fit together and make some sense. But when he applied the question to all the terrible recent events, the answer was always the same: Damien Thorn would benefit.

Only two people now stood between Damien Thorn and total control of the most powerful company in the world: Richard Thorn and his wife.

And Thorn knew instantly why Warren wanted to see him. Warren was going to ask him to kill his brother's son, Damien.

It was Bugenhagen and Robert Thorn all over again. They had tried seven years ago and their efforts had brought them death.

I'm getting carried away again, Thorn thought. I must keep calm. I just stay reasonable. There is too much at stake here.

'You wanna pay and let me get outta here?' asked the cabbie, breaking into Thorn's musings.

Thorn mumbled an apology and reached into his pocket for his wallet. The fare was thirty dollars. Thorn gave the driver another sizable bill to stick around for a while, with the promise of even more if he actually did.

Thorn stepped out of the cab and looked around. He had been brought to an old dilapidated church, standing near the outskirts of a railway yard with tracks originating in faraway Grand Central Station. The church was in great disrepair and looked deserted. Thorn walked up and pushed against the front door. It swung open easily. He turned around to check the cab. It was still by the curb, the engine idling. The driver had pulled his cap over his eyes and already looked asleep. Thorn turned back and went into the building.

The church was as old and musty on the inside as out. The wooden pews were badly scuffed and nearly falling apart. The stained-glass windows had never been washed, and some were broken. Only the distinct smell of incense lingering in the air told Thorn that the church was still in use.

He headed up to the altar. Just as he reached the railing, a door off to his left swung open suddenly, and a small and hunchbacked priest stepped out. 'Mr Thorn?'

Richard nodded.

The priest limped forward and held out his hand. 'I'm Father Weston. Thank you for coming.' He shook Thorn's reluctantly outstretched hand. 'Dr Warren is waiting for you.' He gestured to a side door just to the right of the altar and started limping toward it.

Richard followed. 'Thank you for calling me,' he whispered. 'What's wrong with Dr Warren?'

The priest shook his head. 'He won't talk to me,' he said. 'I only know the man is absolutely terrified.'

They arrived at the small side door, and the priest knocked once.

A hoarse voice came from the other side. 'Who is it?' It didn't sound like Warren at all.

'Mr Thorn is here,' said the priest.

The door swung open, and there stood Warren, looking as though he had been struck by some swift and terrible illness. His eyes were bloodshot and his face hollow, his skin had turned a pale yellow under the stubble of several days' growth of beard. He held a crucifix in his trembling hands. 'Richard?' he asked, in a voice choked with fear.

'It's me, Charles.'

Warren lunged forward. He grabbed Thorn by the collar of his raincoat, dragged him into the room, and slammed the door shut, locking it behind them.

Thorn staggered to maintain his balance. He looked at Warren carefully, certain he was caught in the presence of a madman. 'Charles,' he said placatingly, 'I came as soon as –'

Warren didn't seem to hear him. His wild eyes were focused on something not visible to Thorn. 'The Beast is with us!' he whispered. 'It's true, it's all true! I saw the Wall –'

'Charles, please, listen to me –'

'I saw it! It's horrible!' He shivered and closed his eyes. 'It drove Joan Hart mad, and Bugenhagen –'

Thorn reached forward and grasped Warren by the shoulders. 'Get hold of yourself!' He couldn't believe this was the same man who had so efficiently run his museum for many years, who had been such a good and constant friend. If there was a God in all of this, He certainly wasn't making it easy for those who believed.

Warren stopped shaking. He stared at Thorn as though desperately looking for hope, for an answer. 'Do you believe me now, Richard?' he asked. 'Or do you still think I'm mad?'

Richard continued to hold onto Warren. He didn't want to say he believed, not just yet. One of them had to remain calm and skeptical. But one thing remained to be done. Thorn had to see the Wall.

'Where is it?' he asked finally. 'Where is Yigael's Wall?'

They walked along the railroad tracks, Warren leading the way past a long line of boxcars, some of which carried the Thorn Industries logo. Warren still clutched his crucifix and seemed even more agitated than before. Occasionally he paused to look up at the sky.

'What are you looking for?' asked Thorn.

But Warren was completely agitated again. He could barely speak. Only fragmented mumblings issued from his lips: '. . . not there yet . . . nothing . . . soon . . .'

They finally reached a siding where a lone Thorn Industries container car was parked near the buffers at the end of the track. Warren fumbled with the lock, then motioned for Thorn to go inside.

Thorn turned back to him. 'Aren't you coming in with me?' he asked.

Warren shook his head and looked up at the sky again. He froze in place, absolutely terrified by what he saw.

Thorn followed his gaze. There, in the sky, not more than twenty feet above their heads, an enormous black raven was slowly circling. Richard looked back at Warren, who was now cowering by the railroad car, the crucifix pressed to his chest. 'Come on, Charles,' he said, not comprehending. 'It's only a bird.'

Warren shook his head, keeping his eyes fixed firmly on the raven. He would not move an inch.

Thorn took a deep breath and climbed up into the container car alone.

It was filled with crates of all sizes, all of them packed neatly and tightly – all except one, which had been torn apart halfway, obviously by someone in a great hurry. Thorn went over to look inside.

Meanwhile, in another part of the yard, a long line of heavy cars began shunting backward. The massive wagons bumped noisily into one another as they set themselves in motion, heading in the direction of the lone Thorn Industries container car parked on its separate track.

Outside the car, Warren closed his eyes and started praying. On the adjacent main track, a train suddenly whistled by at a tremendous speed, rattling everything around it and causing Warren to fall to the ground.

He got to his feet and moved toward the front of the car to lean against it and brace himself for whatever was still to come.

Inside the car, Thorn had reached forward and pulled away some of the crate's packing material, until at last he could see a piece of the Wall. The stonelike painted substance looked centuries old, ravaged by time, the colors having faded quite badly. In one section, Thorn's eyes fell upon the likeness of a small child, but here the face was smudged and not clearly defined. Thorn pulled away at more of the packing.

Outside, the massive line of cars continued to pick up speed. They bumped and jerked along, led by a front car with enormous rust-covered points extending menacingly before it. The cars had reached a juncture in the tracks when, suddenly, the tracks switched as though by themselves, and the line of cars began to move into the same track as the one on which the Thorn container car had been parked.

Warren closed his eyes again, as he fervently murmured prayers. Up above, the raven continued to circle, though now with increasing speed and intensity.

Inside the boxcar, Thorn ripped away another section of the crate, revealing a painting of Satan as an adult in his awsome maturity, clinging to the side of a precipice. But this Satan's face was also almost indistinguishable.

Have I gone mad, too? Thorn thought. There is no evidence here.

But just as Damien had been so persistent in searching for the truth about himself, now Richard Thorn was even more persistent in wanting to see all the paintings that covered Yigael's Wall.

He tore back the rest of the crate.

And there before him at last was the face, a face as clear almost as though painted just a few years before. It was a face Thorn knew only too well.

It was the face of Damien Thorn.

There were some differences, of course. Instead of hair, evil, fork-tongued serpents writhed out of the scalp, and instead of human eyes, there were the yellow, slit orbs of a cat. But the face was that of Damien. There was no mistaking it.

Just then the long line of boxcars came barreling toward the single Thorn container car. Warren, absorbed in prayer, opened his eyes in sudden panic, too late to move away from the sharp-pointed tips of the rust-covered prongs on the first car zooming directly toward him. They plunged swiftly into his body, impaling him against the front of the car. He cried out from the horror and excruciating pain, as he hung wriggling from the points, like a living butterfly pinned to a wall.

The crash sent Thorn sprawling to the floor. The Wall behind him started to tip over in his direction. He saw it coming and barely moved out of the way as it crashed down against the floor of the car on the exact spot where he had only a moment before been standing. It splintered into a million tiny pieces.

The evidence he had come so far to discover was gone.

But Thorn did not have time to think about that possible loss. He jumped out of the container car and looked around wildly for his colleague.

Incredibly, Warren was still alive. Blood was beginning to well out of the side of his mouth, and his shirt was soaked with gore where the two rusty points had driven into his chest.

'My God! Charles! Horror stricken, Thorn moved to help his dying friend.

Warren held out one hand feebly, the hand holding the crucifix. 'Take it,' he said in a thin, hoarse whisper. 'And take . . . the daggers.' He struggled for breath. 'The boy . . . must . . . be killed.'

'The daggers?' Thorn asked. 'You have them?'

'Get out,' Warren rasped, 'before it's too late!'

Thorn looked up. The raven was sitting on top of the boxcar, looking down at them with piercing, unflinching eyes. Thorn looked back at Warren. *'Where are the daggers?'* he shouted, fearful now for his own life.

But Warren could no longer hear him. His eyes had rolled back into his head and the crucifix had dropped from his lifeless hand.

Thorn backed away in horror. The raven released a hoarse, ugly cry and lofted up from the boxcar, wheeling around sharply and heading swiftly straight back for Thorn.

Thorn lunged for the crucifix. He grasped the cross, whirled around, shoving it up quickly into the air just a moment before the raven had reached him. The bird screeched savagely and then flew away, circling angrily in the air above him. Thorn moved forward again with the crucifix held high, and the raven moved off. Thorn started to run.

And this time he kept on running.

CHAPTER FOURTEEN

It was the evening of the annual sword-giving ceremony at Davidson Military Academy, the most solemn occasion of the year.

The affair was held in the indoor parade ground; the parents and the rest of the student body were assembled on the balcony, in order to watch the honored cadets below receive the glittering symbols of their achievement.

This year, six cadets were being so honored. Among them was Damien. Mark, too, was to have received a sword, and the five cadets below had spaced themselves in such a way that it was clear one of them was missing. Damien stood in line, very tall and very proud, awaiting his turn. He was still wearing the black band wrapped tightly around his left arm.

Ann stood in the balcony with Buher beside her. She was on the verge of tears. Buher noticed and quickly offered his handkerchief, and Ann took it with a grateful smile.

Down below, a lone bugler stood apart and played as each cadet stepped forward to receive his sword.

On the far side of the balcony a number of pretty young girls were grouped together, all dressed in the same sort of formal gowns, all obviously from the same private school. One stood out in particular – not just because of her fresh and startling beauty, which was considerable, but because of the two formidable men in dark suits who stood directly behind her. Anyone would have realized they were bodyguards, although not everyone would have recognized the girl herself. That was because her father, the governor of Illinois, had made a point of protecting his one and only child from public view.

During the entire ceremony, she never took her eyes off Damien.

When Damien's name was finally called, he stepped forward briskly, almost in a march. He stopped a foot away from the presenter and clicked his heels together smartly, coming to especially sharp attention.

On the balcony, Ann grabbed Buher's arm with a nervousness that was new to her. He patted her hand and smiled reassuringly.

After Damien had received his own sword, the presenter reached for a second one. 'Receive this,' he said, handing the second sword to Damien, 'for your cousin Mark, absent now, but still deserving of this award.'

The crowd burst into spontaneous applause. Ann wiped the ears from her eyes. The governor's daughter across the way applauded more vigorously than anyone else around her.

Damien bowed graciously, then marched back to take his place in the line.

The Thorn chauffeur, Murray, appeared behind Ann on the balcony and whispered something in her ear. She nodded and leaned over to Buher. 'I have to go, Paul. Richard just called from the jet. He's due in any minute now. I want to go meet him at the airport.'

Buher nodded. 'Will you be coming back for the cotillion later?' he asked.

Ann shrugged. 'We'll try,' she said, and left to follow Murray.

Buher watched her leave, then gazed down on the assembly below and caught Neff's eye. Both nodded once, then looked away.

Ann sat in the back of the limousine, anxiously waiting for Richard to deplane. Outside, a wind-whipped Murray was also waiting.

The jet taxied over near the limousine and came to a halt. As soon as the engines were turned off and a set of stairs wheeled against the side, the door flew open and Richard came hurrying down the stairs, taking them two at a time.

He ran over to Murray, without even bothering to wave a hello to Ann. 'Where's Damien?' he asked very tensely.

'At the Academy, sir,' said Murray, confused by Richard's manner.

'We're going to take a cab to the museum. I want you to go get Damien at once and bring him there.' Richard opened up the back door and reached for Ann. 'Come on,' he said, 'you're coming with me.'

The two of them hurried toward the terminal, Ann struggling to keep up with Richard and find out what in heaven's name was going on. Murray looked after them, a sudden hatred burning in his eyes.

The cotillion was well underway. The boys and girls swirling around on the dance floor looked wonderfully old-fashioned. The cadets were dressed in formal uniform, while most of the young girls wore floor-length white gowns and corsages.

Over against the far wall, near the table with the punchbowl, stood those who were not dancing, either out of shyness or disinterest; girls off to one side, boys off to the other. Although they exchanged glances and giggled, they made no other overtures.

In another part of the room, Damien stood with Sergeant Neff, both watching the dancers. Across the room was the young girl with the two bodyguards. She was looking at Damien with interest, and Neff took notice. 'You'll need courage to dance with *her*,' he said.

185

'The governor's daughter?' asked Damien. He knew exactly what Neff meant.

Neff nodded.

Damien smiled. 'You forget I know the family,' he said, and proceeded to walk across the room.

As Neff watched, a satisfied look came into his eyes.

Richard was rushing through the main floor of the museum, heading for the stairs that led to the basement. Ann was fast upon is heels.

'You can't make me believe it!' she said breathlessly, trying to catch up.

'You've *got* to believe it!' he said. 'He killed Mark. He killed Atherton, and Pasarian –'

'Stop it!' she cried, finally catching up and grabbing his arm.

Richard turned on her. 'He'll go on killing. He'll kill anyone he thinks is endangering him.' He broke away from Ann's grasp and headed down the wide marble stairs leading to the basement level.

Ann was furious. 'How?' she asked. 'How did he kill them? Did he make the ice crack –'

'No,' said Richard, 'not by himself –'

'Or tear the gas pipe apart?'

Richard stopped in his tracks and looked at her. 'There are others,' he said, 'surrounding him, helping him. Keeping him safe!'

Ann swallowed hard. She could not believe she was actually hearing her husband say these things. 'Richard,' she said, attempting to seem calm. 'listen to yourself. Listen to how crazy you sound! "Others"? More devils? A conspiracy of devils? Richard, *please*!'

Richard grabbed hold of her hands. 'Ann,' he said, pleading with her to believe him, 'I saw Charles killed –'

Ann gasped. This was the first mention of Charles's death.

'And I saw *Damien's face* on Yigael's Wall!'

186

There was a long, suspenseful moment. The two of them faced each other in a terrific battle of wills – Richard wanting so much for her to believe him, Ann wanting so much for Richard to take it all back, to admit it was all some sort of terrible joke.

But it wasn't a joke, and Ann was terrified at the thought of what was still going to happen. 'What are you going to do?' she asked in a hushed voice, a voice quivering with fear.

Damien was dancing with the governor's daughter, and doing beautifully. The girl seemed to be having the time of her life. All of the boys watched them in awe, and most of the girls were filled with jealousy. The two of them really did make a wonderfully attractive young couple.

After a turn around the dance floor, Damien finally noticed Neff and Murray, deep in conversation on the far side of the room. The chauffeur caught Damien's eye.

'Excuse me,' Damien said very politely, 'I'll be right back.' He walked the governor's daughter back to her escorts and then went over to join Murray and Neff.

As he approached them, Neff stepped toward him and said very quietly, 'Be careful.'

Damien looked at him with cold disdain and replied, 'You forget who I am.'

Neff bowed his head as though in respectful apology.

Damien turned on his heel and left, following Murray to the limousine waiting outside.

When Richard finally found the key he was looking for and unlocked the door to Warren's office, he burst into the room, switched on the light, and immediately started to search frantically, opening and shutting drawers, cabinets, looking under objects, under tables.

'What are you doing?' asked Ann, standing in the doorway.

Richard looked up and said very distinctly, 'The daggers are here. They *must* be.'

Ann rushed into the room. 'Richard, no!' she cried. 'Don't! I won't let you –'

Richard pushed her away. 'Get away!' he said. 'I know they're here somewhere.'

Ann was now growing wild with fear. 'You're going to *kill* him!'

Richard kept looking. 'He's got to be –'

'*No!*'

'Ann, the boy isn't human!' He finally came upon the locked drawer and fiercely tugged at it.

'He's your brother's son!' Ann said, starting to cry. 'You've loved him for seven years as if he were your own!'

But Richard wasn't listening to her. He was determined to get the drawer open, and he couldn't. He glanced desperately around for some kind of tool and caught sight of a tray filled with archaeological digging equipment. He grabbed the chisel and turned back toward the drawer.

Outside the limousine pulled to a stop in front of the museum. Damien let himself out, leaned back in to say something quickly to Murray, and then jogged up the steps, taking them two at a time.

CHAPTER FIFTEEN

'Wait, Richard!' Ann pleaded. 'Please, for me, wait!'

But her words fell upon deaf ears, because Richard had finally wrenched open the drawer; he stood there gazing with a strange perverse satisfaction at the daggers, all seven of them, gleaming in the cold overhead light.

Damien, meanwhile, jogged down the wide marble stairs which led from the lobby to the basement. In the far distance ahead of him, it was possible to hear muffled voices – the voice of Ann pleading, and that of Richard, resisting. Damien's face, however, was expressionless. And he kept right on walking.

Ann had lunged forward to shut the drawer, throwing herself between Richard and the menacing daggers. 'I won't let you!' she screamed.

Richard stared back at her. 'Give me the daggers, Ann.'

She shook her head, tears beginning to stream down her cheeks.

'Ann.' He spoke very slowly, emphasizing every word. 'Give – them – to – me.'

They stared at each other for what seemed an eternity. Finally she dropped her gaze from his and turned around haltingly, as though a great, shattering sadness had taken over her heart. Slowly, slowly, she pulled open the drawer.

Damien was now standing directly outside the door leading to Warren's office, listening intently, concentrating almost as though in a trance. He had shut his eyes and had begun to tremble.

189

Once again Ann seemed to hesitate. She moved with a dreadful sense of purpose, as though struggling to stop herself from what she was being directed to do. Was there a voice inside her far more powerful than her own feeble will? She reached into the drawer and pulled out the cluster of daggers. And then she turned back to face her husband.

Richard held out his hands for the knives.

Suddenly Ann moved forward, as though possessed with a strange new demonic power. Her face had become evil, twisted, horribly altered into that of a madwoman. She leaned close to Richard's ear and whispered, *'Here, Richard, here are your daggers,'* as she plunged all seven of the blades deep into his body.

His eyes opened wide in shock and horror. 'Ann!' he cried out, as his body fell forward, smashing against the floor, the fall forcing the blades to cruelly pierce his body.

Ann tossed back her head with a gesture of triumph, her eyes closed, her mouth framed in a joyous smile, and then she screamed out one shattering word.

'DAMIEN!'

Damien had stopped trembling, and he opened his eyes. He reached out for the doorknob, then hesitated, as though something had forced him to change his mind. He stood there quietly for a while, as if in deep concentration. And then, very softly and quickly, he turned and moved back toward the stairs.

In the boiler room, which was directly adjacent to Warren's workshop, the largest furnace units began to rumble ominously . . .

In the workshop, Ann stood quite still, as though suspended in a trance of joy.

Damien began to walk away faster.

It was then the furnace exploded in the nearby room. A jet of burning oil sprayed through the connecting heat vents into the workshop, drenching Ann as she stood

190

transfixed in her moment of glory. She screamed as the oil burst into flames, turning her into a blazing torch.

Damien, as though his mission were accomplished, quickly crossed the lobby upstairs. All around him, the museum's alarm system, triggered by the fire below, began its defeafening clanging.

And then the sprinkler system finally burst, enveloping Ann's body in a cloud of steam.

Too late.

Joyous in her flaming death, like some demonic Joan of Arc, she lifted her face toward the heavens and cried out, 'Damien! *Damien*! *DAMIEN*!'

At the front door of the museum, Damien paused and looked back, a semblance of sorrow filling his eyes. And then he pushed open the door and went into the night.

Stretched out before him lay the great city of Chicago, still glowing brightly in the clear night sky. Far off in the distance came the wailing sound of fire engines, speeding to fight the holocaust threatening to destroy the famed Thorn Museum.

Down below the entrance, the sleek black Thorn limousine awaited him. Murray, ever the efficient chauffeur, stood erect beside the opened passenger door on the right side.

Damien trotted down the wide steps fronting the museum building and quickly ducked into the back of the car.

There, sitting comfortably in the dark interior, were Paul Baher and Sergeant Neff, both smiling and looking satisfied.

Damien signaled the chauffeur to start the car. As the limousine slipped quietly away into the night, the young man named Damien once more looked out the back window toward the museum, which was now nearly consumed by the fire. The blaze reflected onto the car's

191

windows, and across Damien's face, which bore a look of delight at the flickering dance of the flames.

And Damien smiled.

> *For such are false apostles, deceitful workers, transforming themselves into the Apostles of Christ. And no marvel; for Satan himself is transformed into an Angel of Light.* (2 Corinthians 11: 13)